GIRL ON FIRE

GEMMA AMOR

This is a work of fiction. Names, characters, businesses, places, events and incidents are either the products of the author's imagination or used in a fictitious manner.
Any resemblance to actual persons, living or dead, or actual events is purely coincidental.

Girl on Fire
First Edition October 2020

Cover illustration by Chris Panatier
Cover wraparound design by Gemma Amor
Formatting by Ross Jeffery

ISBN: 9798638058197
ASIN: B08HNG1FW3

CONTENTS

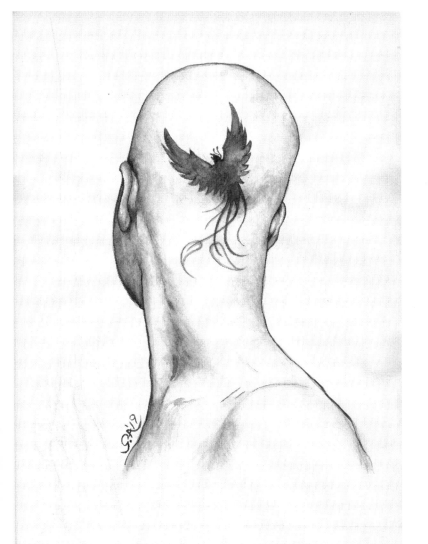

RUBY

When I was a kid, my Daddy took me for a walk in the woods behind our house one afternoon. This was before I learned not to trust my Daddy, or go anywhere alone with him if I could help it.

This was before I learned how to hate.

'Ruby,' he said, as we walked through the trees, listening to the birds. It was sunny, I remember that. I remember crickets in the grass. I remember the feel of my summer dress brushing against my legs. It had flowers on it. They were blue cornflowers, I think. It was my favourite dress. It was Daddy's favourite dress, too.

I burned it, later.

'Yeah, Daddy?' I said, holding his hand and trying to match his pace. He always walked fast, leaning forward at the waist like he was hinged, hinged and constantly about to snap shut, like a bear trap. I had no idea why Daddy was always like that, why he always moved as if holding himself together through force of will alone. I had no idea why he was always so angry. It was just a part of who he was, like his hair, sandy and thick, and his arms, strong and corded with muscle, and his fingernails, which he always kept immaculately manicured.

Abruptly, he stopped, let go of my hand, and took me by the shoulders, gripping me hard, those perfectly tended fingernails digging into my soft skin through the fabric of the dress. We stared at each other. There was something weird and dark and intense about his expression. His pupils were too big. He was breathing heavily.

'What is it, Daddy?' I said, confused, and a little scared.

'People are trash, Ruby,' he replied, pushing his face close to mine, so close that his eyes grew huge, merging together over the bridge of his nose into one massive, furious orb. I remember the smell of him, that day. Musky and sour and unpleasant. Looking back, I'm fairly certain he was drunk, but at the time, I was too small to know that.

Looking back, that was the first time I felt truly afraid of him.

He shook me a little, and my head whipped about like a rag doll's. It hurt, and I cried out in pain, but he ignored me.

'Don't you ever forget that, you hear, Ruby?!' He said, savagely. I saw sweat gathering on his top lip. It made me feel sick, although I didn't know why.

'People. Are. Trash.'

'Okay, Daddy,' I replied, fighting back tears. He showed no immediate signs of easing his grip. He just kept staring at me until he was sure that I'd gotten the message. Then, eventually, he let go.

And we carried on walking, as if nothing had happened.

But it had. Something had happened. Something big. A change in him. An awakening, perhaps. It worried me. It felt like something inside of Daddy got sprung, at last. The trap had been triggered. The jaws had finally snapped shut, and I didn't realise, until much later, that they had snapped down on me.

And from that day on, every single morning, without fail, Daddy would leave the house to go to work and point at me as he walked through the kitchen and towards the front door.

'What do we need to remember, Ruby?' He'd say, and I wouldn't be able to make eye-contact with him.

'People are trash, Daddy,' I'd reply, obediently, staring at my cereal instead as it slowly dissolved in a bowl of yellowing milk.

'And don't you forget it,' he'd demand, and the door would close behind him, and I would keep on eating my cereal, and the echo of the words would bounce around inside my skull:

People are trash, people are trash, people…

Are.

Trash.

I'm not sure I believed him or really understood what he was saying, in the beginning. They were just words, and words don't mean much on their own without context.

But, if you say something enough times in a row, eventually, you start to believe it, even if it once started out as a lie. They call it 'positive reinforcement' or some such horseshit. 'People are trash,' said Daddy, every single day, for years and years, and, over time, as I grew older, I saw that he was right. I got the context. It came when I was fifteen and Daddy locked himself into my bedroom one afternoon when school was finished and Mom was out and we were alone in the house. I realised, afterwards, after he'd excused himself and left me alone, that *he* was trash, too.

Context.

I tried to tell people when it first started. I tried to tell Mom, but she shouted at me and told me to stop spreading disgusting lies around about my Daddy. I tried to tell my teacher at school, but I lost my nerve when he began to talk over me, telling me that I 'needed to focus on my grades' and 'the future wouldn't wait for me to make my mind up about what I wanted from life,' and I never even got three words out in a row. I tried, eventually, to tell the cops, anonymously, going so far as to take the bus to the local police station, but then I got scared that someone would see me going inside, someone would tell Daddy, because our town was the kind of place where everyone knew everyone's business, private or otherwise, and I found I couldn't go through with it. And so it became less about context, and more about keeping a dirty, shameful secret, not because I *wanted* to keep the secret, but because I couldn't give it away, couldn't make it an open truth.

Instead, I internalised it, just like Daddy internalised his own gangrenous rage until it bubbled out of him in sordid dribs and drabs: a squeeze here, a questing, well-manicured finger there, a slap on something tender and unsuspecting. Teeth, sometimes, and tongue. *Daddy is trash,* I told myself, silently, while he did this, *Daddy hurts me.* And I stopped trying to tell people what they didn't want to hear, and just started telling them what they did.

'I'm okay,' I would say, when asked. 'I feel peachy.'

But it wasn't.

And I didn't.

And this is what you get, I guess, when context takes over. A world full of trash people, walking around, polluting everything in sight. Piles of garbage, a garbage kingdom. It makes my skin crawl. It makes me angry. I am *so* angry, all the fucking time, and I don't know how to do anything about it. I don't *want* to do anything about it. My anger is fuel. My anger gives me focus. My anger is *who I am.* If I let it go, what's left? Nothing. A pathetic shell of a person who had bad things done to her. Who wants to be that person? A victim. I don't. Fuck that. Forgiveness is weak. Acceptance is weak. Moving on is weak.

Owning the anger, though, living it with every breath...now that feels honest, somehow.

Because it is clear to me, clearer than anything has been for a long time, that I have a purpose. I have been brought back from the dead for a reason. A mission.

To clear the world of trash.

And how do we get rid of trash?

We burn it.

We burn it all.

My car is old, and shit. Old, shit and yet so, so beautiful. It's a cherry red 1989 Pontiac Bonneville. It's the first car I've ever owned, and will probably be the only car I'll ever want to own. I saved every paycheck from my first regular job to buy it. I got no help from the bank of Mom or Dad. This car is a symbol of my independence, my freedom. I love it more than anything, or anyone.

The engine throbs as I put my foot down on the accelerator. I have my window open, as the car is too old for functioning air con. My red hair whips around my head as I push down with my foot. Red hair, red car. The needle creeps to seventy-five. Seventy-five, and I feel alive. I feel happy. There is country music on the radio. Around me, the dry, arid plains of Nevada stretch out into the distance. The asphalt highway slices through the middle of it all like an arrow, pointing to my future. They call this 'the loneliest road in America'. Well, I don't know about that, but it sure is one of the prettiest. In the distance, mountains loom.

Overhead, a blue sky stretches out into infinity. A hot sun burns in the blue.

I am free. I throw my arms up in the air, letting go of the wheel for a moment, unable to restrain myself any longer. I crow, and yell out joyously. My voice is whipped away like a dry leaf on the breeze.

'Wooooooooo-hooooooo!'

I try to push the needle further around the dial, and the engine starts to protest, unused to this kind of speed. I'm not going to win any races with this car, but this is faster than I've ever driven it before, and my baby isn't sure about it. It's more used to crawling around the city than my current pedal-to-the-metal style of driving.

'Come on baby, you can do it,' I croon, and then I scream again, unable to keep it inside me, this joy: 'Yeahhhhhh!'

The car races faster along the road. I throw my arms up once more, fists clenched tight, punching out, victorious, queen of the fucking world.

And then, it happens. There is a *bang!* And a jolt. My car has hit a pothole in the road, a pothole I could not have seen, because I am driving too fast.

I am thrown sideways. My head whacks the window frame hard on my right-hand side. I am not holding the wheel, so I can't control the sudden swerving of the car as both tyres on my right-hand side burst. I feel the rims of each wheel scrape along the ground. They make a hideous noise. The car begins to veer wildly off the road.

Panicked, I finally manage to grab hold of the steering wheel and yank it over hard to the left to try to correct my trajectory, but this only sends me further off. The car speeds towards the verge of the road. The road is raised higher than the surrounding land, only by a small measurement, but enough to create a ledge between the asphalt and the scrubby green plants that poke up through the sand all around.

Me and my car hit the ledge, still doing seventy. I slam my foot on the brakes, but it's too late. The car squeals as if in agony, then shoots off the road and into the desert.

There is a moment, a split second when I think everything is going to be okay, that the car will stop, dragged to a halt by the sand and the scrub.

The car will stop.

It will all be okay.

Instead, my car, my baby, unable to cope with the drop in ground level, tilts dangerously onto its side, flips, and then rolls down the slight incline away from the highway.

My world is turned literally upside down, and then right way up, and then wrong way down again. I am strapped into my seat. I put my arms up, not in joy, now, but in fear, for protection, and brace myself against the roof of the car. I am dimly aware that I am screaming, that blood is dripping down my face from where my head hit the window frame.

The car rolls two, three times, and then comes to an uneasy rest, leaving me suspended upside down, and half unconscious.

Gradually, the dust settles around me. The car creaks and moans in pain, as do I. I hang from my seatbelt, my head squashed uncomfortably against the roof, which is now the floor.

A stillness falls. Blood begins to pound in my ears. I lack the energy to try to unstrap myself. I'm afraid I might hurt myself if I try.

I call out, knowing it is futile. This is the loneliest road in America, after all.

'Help!' I whimper, to the empty world. Then, slightly louder: 'Please, someone, help me!'

It's a waste of my time, my energy. I stop, feeling faint. I close my eyes and try to find the strength to undo my seatbelt. I can't. The full weight of my body is hanging downwards, pressing against the belt, locking the mechanism. It won't budge. I start to pant, and panic, and then I faint, black out momentarily.

Gradually, I am woken again, this time by a sound. Well, two sounds, actually. The first is the unmistakably wet noise of something liquid trickling out of my car and into the sand.

Fuel.

The second is a hissing, juddering, fizzing sort of noise coming from underneath the hood of the Pontiac. I have a moment to wonder what this means.

The upper intake's gonna go, I think fuzzily. Faulty fuel pressure regulator? Punctured... engine... wall?

What the hell am I talking about? I don't know shit about cars. I have no idea.

Daddy would know.

Wait, no, don't think about Daddy, not now. Focus.

Focus!

Then, the car explodes.

A WALL of fire and heat blasts against my face. A fireball envelops the car.

I am screaming.

I am burning.

I am burning!

First, my clothes. Then, my hair, which disappears in a flash, curling crazily first and then simply melting away. The stench of my own flesh roasting is unbearable. Everything around me is red, orange, black. The roaring of the fire is so intense, so loud, so terrible, and I am in the middle of it all, I am the fire, I am the eye of the fucking storm. I open my mouth to scream again, but this one is wordless, and the fire invades me, licking the back of my throat, filling me up from the inside out.

It is too much. It is too much. Pain. Burning.

I close my eyes.

I die.

OR, not. Slowly, carefully, disbelievingly, I open each eye. I am lying in a blackened heap of ash, and twisted metal, and scorched earth. The charred skeleton of my car rises from the desert like a sad, ancient shipwreck rises from the sea-bed: an echo of a life that once was. A blackened footprint in time.

A memory of the old me.

I see smoke, dark and noxious, curling up into the sky. Small, residual fires burn in a few places on the scrubland around the car wreckage. They glow a muted orange, little distress signals that no one can see except for me. I focus on my body, trying to assess how injured I am. I can't feel anything wrong.

How is that possible?

I am curled up like a newborn, tucked into the foetal position, arms and hands clasped to my chest, knees drawn up to my chin.

There is no pain, none of the pain I expected at any rate. No burning, no bleeding, no broken bones.

A thin, keening cry sounds out overhead. I blearily look at the sky, and see the outlines of birds circling my body, vultures, or crows, I can't tell: my vision is still blurred, misty, my eyes raw from heat and smoke.

I unfurl like a reluctant flower, slowly, cautiously, still reeling from the shock and the impact of the crash.

A thought worms its way into the front of my mind.

How am I still alive?

How can anyone survive an explosion like that?

I shiver with the cold, and it dawns on me that I am naked, that my clothes have burned clean away. If I stay here, lying on the ground, I will freeze. Nights in the desert get real cold, real fast.

I stand, the remains of my car, my life, scattered around my feet. I can still feel the heat from the blaze. I hold my arms out in front of me, inspecting my flesh in the rapidly fading light.

No burns, no blisters, no scars. I run a hand over myself, up each arm, over my belly, my legs, and finally up over my head. The hair on my head and my body has gone, leaving behind a fine, fuzzy stubble. Otherwise, I'm untouched.

Completely unscathed.

And alone.

Unsure of what else to do, I start to walk unsteadily along the road, back the way I had driven only a few hours earlier. I see the pothole I hit whilst driving too fast, whilst waving my arms in the air like an idiot instead of holding the steering wheel. It's small, but the edges are jagged. I stare at it, and then move on. It is in the past now. What has happened has happened.

What matters is what comes next.

And clothes. God, I need some clothes. I throw a last, longing look at the wreckage of my old car over my shoulder as I walk away, and feel my heart breaking a little in my chest. I have no idea what is happening to me, or how, or why, but I know there is no going back from this.

There is no going back to who I was before.

I am a Phoenix from the ashes, but what that means for my future, I have no idea. I face forward, walking slowly along the highway, headed towards I don't know what.

IT ISN'T long before I hear the sound of engines approaching. I know enough about motors to recognise the sound of multiple Harley-Davidson twin-cams roaring towards me. Bikers. Four of them, riding side-by-side, hogging the highway, as bikers do.

Moments later I am illuminated by the glare of headlights, and a cavalcade of Harleys surround me, engines chewing up the night air.

They slow, and then stop, putting down the kickstands, removing helmets, leaning on their handlebars, assessing me. There are three men and one woman. They are heavily tattooed, and look like they belong to a gang.

They stare at my naked, shivering body. I put a hand up to protect my eyes from the glare of the headlights.

The leader of the gang dismounts, and walks over to me, heavy boots jingling slightly as he moves. He pulls a cigar from his jacket pocket and lights it with a zippo covered in skulls. Skull rings gleam on his fingers. There are roses choked with thorns tattooed on his face. Entwined with the roses, a green snake, which winds down his neck and vanishes under his wife-beater.

He lights the cigar and continues to peer at me, a slow, predatory smile spreading across his face.

'Well,' he says, looking me up and down. 'Just what do we have here?'

I work my dry mouth, not sure how well my voice will work. 'Please,' I say, hoping against vain hope that this isn't all about to go horribly wrong. 'Please. I was in an accident. My car... it... came off the road.' I pointed back up the highway behind me.

'I need help. Clothes, water... anything. Please.'

The biker laughs, and it isn't kind. My heart sinks.

'Help? Yeah, I can see that. You need a lot of help, girl.'

The others laugh with him, and my neck prickles: a warning sign. I know the look on this man's face. I know it from my life before the Pontiac. I know it from all the nights I couldn't sleep when I was younger, couldn't sleep for knowing what was coming. I know it like I know the skin on the back of my hands. I don't remember much about my childhood, not the same way most people remember things, but I do remember the first time I saw that look on the face of another man, and I think the expression is "Out of the frying pan, and into the fire," except I've already been in the fire, and now I am here.

I turn my attention to the only woman in the group, trying to ignore how the men leer at my naked body, eyes lingering on my breasts and ass, hungry. I need clothes, and I need to get away from these people, quickly.

'Please,' I plead with the female biker who looks at me like I'm an alien. 'I don't want any trouble. I just want to cover myself up. Even just a blanket, a scarf. Anything. Please.'

I shouldn't have to grovel like this, but I am desperate, my body quivering. The words fall on her and slide off like rain down a windowpane.

She narrows her eyes, and sneers at me.

'Do I look like a fucking charity service, bitch?'

I am taken aback by the malevolence in her voice. A memory of my mother's face flashes into view. I had tried to tell her something she didn't want to hear, once, and her face had looked just like this woman's.

What does a girl have to fucking do to get some help in this world?

Mom later told me to never rely on others, to only look out for yourself. *Easier said than done,* I think, looking around at the crew surrounding me.

The leader speaks up, amused.

'Now, Violet, no need to be like that. We can help out this little lady, can't we? What do you say, boys? Shall we... help her out?'

I know what is coming next.

I turn and try to run, but the leader catches me around the waist easily, throwing me to the ground.

'Oh, don't be like that, missy,' he says, kneeling in the sand next to my naked body.

'See, the way I look at it, we can help you out just fine. But things in this life don't come for free, understand me?'

He starts fumbling with his fly, unzipping it with a degree of ceremony that speaks to his opinion of his own virility. He holds me pinned to the ground easily with his other arm, and as he continues to fumble with himself, the other two men in his gang join us on the dirt, taking my arms and my legs, holding me firm. I struggle and buck and squeal, but that only excites them more, and they start crowing, and guffawing, and grunting the more I try to escape.

The leader's eyes are hot with excitement.

'Nothing comes for free, like I said, missy. So, I can help you, sure. But you gotta help me first, alright?'

And all I can think is: *No.*

Not again.

Oh Christ, not again.

No.

I said I would never let it happen again!

NEVER!

The man's face moves close to mine, and he drags his thick, wet tongue down my cheek.

NO!

And that's when I feel it.

It starts in my fingertips, which grow hot, so hot my skin begins to hum, to vibrate. The heat travels up my arms, down my chest and spreads to my legs. I have a moment to see something burning and red reflected in the man's eyes, which have widened in shock.

And then I explode, like a fucking volcano.

For the second time that day I am on fire, but this time... I do not burn.

Flames spurt out of every orifice, fire roaring up into what is now the night sky in great, twisting columns, a tornado of fire, a goddamn pyre, born of rage and pain and anger at where I find myself, held down by three disgusting horny fuck-pigs, men who would rather rape a woman in trouble than help her out a little. Why do people like to do shit like this to each other? Why? Why are all the people I meet the bad people, instead of the good? *Are* there any good people?

Well, fuck them.

Fuck them *all*.

Through the sound of the fire I can hear all three of the men screaming in agony, and it only makes me burn brighter. I burn and burn until their faces melt clean off their skulls, until their bones lie around me like blackened sticks. The scent of charcoal and cooked meat is thick in the air. I savour it.

The flames die down, slowly, slowly, and I stand. The desert is quiet, peaceful almost. I feel lighter, although suddenly overwhelmed with tiredness.

I have just killed three men. I clench my fists.

They fucking deserved it, though.

I look over to where the Harleys are parked. The female biker, Violet, is still sitting astride her bike, immobilised with fear, her face white, her mouth open. I walk towards her with heavy, measured paces.

She fumbles for something, brings up a gun, and shoots at me before I have time to react.

'Stay away, you fucking freak!' she shouts, and shoots again. Both bullets hit me square in the chest. I should die, right now, and bleed out on the sand. But I know I won't.

I am the fucking Phoenix.

Nothing can kill me.

I watch with a detached curiosity as the bullets work their way out of my chest and fall to the ground, glowing white hot.

I must be made of fire now, I think.

Does it fill my veins? If you cut me, do I not burn?

I start to chuckle, and then throw my head back and laugh aloud, hurling my mirth into the night like an offering.

Violet stares at me, lowers the gun, and starts to cry.

'Shut up,' I say, sternly now, my laughter subsiding. 'Shut up and give me your clothes.' She obeys. I dress in borrowed leather, order the pathetic creature off of her bike, and mount the Harley, from the left side. My brother had a bike like this once, back when life was simpler. I know how to ride.

I start the engine. I feel the Harley throb underneath me. I feel the weight of the bike, the weight of my own actions. I warm up to the bike and it warms up to me.

The now naked biker shivers and sobs in the dirt at my feet, where she belongs. I hold a hand out, not really knowing what I'm doing, but trying it anyway. After a moment, a small, campfire-sized blaze springs up from the ground next to her. It will keep her warm until the morning.

Then, she's on her own.

'Don't leave me out here with them,' she croaks, throwing a sickened look at her former gang mates. There's not much of them left to look at.

She should consider herself lucky, really.

I put up the kickstand, rev the engine. I cannot resist a final word.

'Do I look like a fucking charity service, Violet?' I say, relishing each word, and then I drive away into the night.

Before all this madness, I'd been headed for the mountains. Time to head for the mountains again.

Second time lucky.

I drive until the Harley runs out of fuel, then I ditch it, and set it alight so no-one can track me. Then I steal another bike, or car, or whatever I can get hold of, and continue until that vehicle runs out of gas, and repeat the cycle. I figure it isn't a good idea to refuel. I don't have any money, and I'm paranoid about someone spotting my stolen ride, calling it in. I do not want to be found. I never want to be found, ever again.

Besides, I also figure that the new, flammable version of me and a gas station are perhaps not such a great combination.

I have a destination in mind. I have a plan, too. I am going to rebuild my life.

You see, back when I was in my Pontiac, driving through the bright afternoon sun, I was happy about it for a reason. I was leaving my home behind, and my family. I was escaping the prison that had held me captive for so many years.

Most importantly, I was leaving Daddy behind, for good, this time.

For the first time in my life, as I drove too fast along that desert highway, I had felt truly free.

I see no reason for the status quo to change now that I've died, and risen from the ashes.

It's symbolic, really. Out with the old, and in with the new.

My destination is North, as far away from my birth town as it's possible to get without actually leaving the States. I have a place in mind, and I plan on getting a job in a bar, or wherever will take me. I plan on setting up on my own. I plan on never having to rely on anyone else ever again.

Day turns to night, and night to day, and I am driving. Driving until Nevada merges into Idaho, getting through car after car after bike after truck.

I don't seem to need to eat anymore, or sleep. I do however get thirsty. The irony of this is not lost on me. I seem to always be fighting off dehydration, and I get terrible headaches if I don't drink at least a litre of water every hour. There is only so much water a person can travel with, so I end up stopping more than I am comfortable with. Most roadside places I pass allow me a glass of tap water, which I drink quickly, head down, staring at the counter, avoiding all eye contact. I issue a brisk 'Thanks' and leave as quietly as I arrive.

I manage two weeks of this before the Police catch up with me.

Well, one Policeman.

JUST OFF HIGHWAY 26, there is a small town called Glenns Ferry. It's sparsely littered with cutesy wooden houses and an old livery barn. It's the kind of place where large, old guys in dungarees hang out on street corners all day, chewing the fat. There's a rail crossing right in the middle of the town. Directly opposite those train tracks is the uninviting Oregon Trail Cafe & Bar.

It's in this bar that Officer Bright finds me.

I am sitting hunched over a table in a corner, my back to the room. I'm still in my borrowed leathers, which fit me surprisingly well. I like them, they feel like armour against the vagaries of the world. Officer Bright sits down at my table, uninvited. I know his name is Bright because it's stitched to his lapel badge. He finds me in the middle of making a really terrible decision: to drink beer instead of water, in an attempt to find a little liquid satisfaction on such a hot day. Sometimes, water just doesn't cut it like cold suds do.

There is a collection of four empty bottles on the oiled red gingham tablecloth between us, and I'm just about to finish my fifth. I am beginning to realise that beer has a bad effect on my new body. It makes me feel mean, real mean, and loose with it, too. My fingertips are already starting to buzz when Officer Bright takes off his sunglasses and tries to establish eye contact with me.

'Ruby?' he says, softly. 'Ruby Miller?'

There's no point trying to deny it. He takes an old photograph out of his jacket pocket, slides it across the table to me. It's a school photo from a few years back. My thick red hair is the main feature of the picture, and I am hiding behind it as much as humanly possible. I was shy in school.

I don't feel shy anymore.

I turn and beckon to the waitress, who shuffles over.

'Yeah?' she drawls, rudely. 'Can I getcha?'

I ask for more beer, ignoring the Policeman, and she obliges, shuffling off while grumbling under her breath, looking between me and Officer Bright with a verminous breed of curiosity. She yanks a beer out of an old, dirty fridge, shuffles back across the room, pops the lid off a bottle and hands it to me.

'Shall I put it on your tab?' she asks, and then blows a bubble with the blob of gum she's been chewing since I got here. The bubble pops, and I grit my teeth.

People.

People are trash, Ruby, a voice says in my head.

It isn't my voice.

'Sure,' I reply, taking the beer. Condensation beads the glass, and instantly sizzles as it hits the hot skin of my fingers. The policeman notices this, and frowns. He then shakes his head slightly, dismisses it as a trick of the light, or a figment of his imagination.

I slowly meet his gaze, and let just a little, tiny ember glow in each of my eyes. He blinks, and then opens his mouth, resolute.

'Are you Ruby Miller?' He asks, flatly.

'It's not a crime to leave home,' I say, not answering him directly. 'I'm an adult. I can leave without it being a Police matter.'

He narrows his eyes. 'True. But I'm not interested in you running away, although your Mother is beside herself with worry. Nope.' He sighs, and fiddles with the label on an empty bottle of bud, gearing up.

'No,' he continues, heavily, 'I'm interested in the burned out wreckage of one abandoned Pontiac, a 1989 Bonneville, very distinctive, and registered to you. And, I'm interested in the three abandoned Harleys we found close by, back on a certain highway in Nevada.'

There is silence as I listen and sip my beer.

'I'm also interested in the remains of the three men we found near those bikes, remains we had to ID with dental records, because those remains were no more than cinders and ash. Not to mention the naked woman we found near dead from exposure not half a mile away. She kept shouting about a... girl on fire. 'Girl on fire!' she screamed at us, over and over again. She's in the hospital now. But we showed her your picture, and she recognised you. Despite the...haircut.'

He gestures at my bald head. The hair that burned away has not regrown, but I am fine with it. It's a lot easier to manage. I am thinking about getting a tattoo across my scalp, of a phoenix, but I don't know how my new skin will respond to this.

My fingers tingle again with heat, and my beer bottle cracks suddenly, the glass unable to cope with the rapid shift from cold to hot. The contents of the bottle dump themselves all over the table with a definitive splash, and then spread, trickling over the edge of the table and onto Officer Bright.

The cop jumps, looks down at his suddenly wet lap, and narrows his eyes.

Otherwise, he keeps his composure.

I'm almost impressed.

'One more thing,' he says, in a carefully neutral voice. The cop shifts in his seat, wet and uncomfortable, but committed, as a man of the law should be. The beer starts dripping onto the linoleum floor all around us. The gentle splashing reminds me of the noise my car made as it leaked fuel into the desert that fateful day when I burned for the first time.

'We can't seem to find your Daddy anywhere,' he says.

We stare at each other over the spilled beer, a show-down at high noon.

There is no point denying it.

I have no wish to deny it.

I had every right to do what I did.

I fold my arms.

'They were going to rape me,' I say, calm as you like. 'I needed help, and they held me down, and tried to violate me instead. All of them.'

Officer Bright's eyes flicker with sympathy, and then harden. He shifts in his seat again, carefully. He is preparing himself to make a move.

'Be that as it may,' he says gravely, 'I have no choice. You're wanted on suspicion of three counts of homicide, and one count of arson.' He slowly reaches to his belt, produces a pair of handcuffs. 'And we really need to talk about your Daddy.'

Fierce pain stabs at my heart.

Talk about my Daddy, he says.

Talk about...

My.

Daddy.

And say what, exactly?

Where would I even start?

I glare at him, and he sighs.

'It would help me out greatly if you'd oblige me by coming outside.'

'No,' I say.

He stands up. 'Ruby Miller,' he says, moving towards me, and reaching out to take my arm. 'I'm arresting you on...'

I hold up my hand to stop him, and my fingers catch fire. He snatches his own backwards in shock. I twist and turn my wrist and my fingers, playing with the flames lovingly.

'No,' I repeat.

His eyes grow wide, and his mouth drops open.

'How are you doing that?' he whispers, and I am dimly aware that the rest of the room has grown deathly silent.

I shrug. 'I don't know. It happened after I crashed my car. But that's not important. What's important is that things can get real hot, real quick. And I don't want to hurt you. You're just doing your job. But I will burn this whole fucking town down if I have to.'

Hopefully he can see from the expression on my face that I am deadly serious.

'I made a promise to myself, Officer. A man once kept me a prisoner, for years, in my own home. He called himself my Daddy, and thought that gave him free reign to do whatever he wanted to me, if you catch my drift. So I resolved to never let another man lay a hand on me again, unless I wish it so. And to never be holden to another person, or to other people's rules, for the rest of my life. So you see, I can't come with you. Those men tried to rape me. They got justice for that. I'm guilty, but I'm sure as fuck not going to jail for it. What would be the point? I'd just raze the whole place to the ground, anyway.'

The confusion on Officer Bright's face is palpable, and I feel almost sorry for him.

'I'll tell you what's going to happen now,' I say, and wish I hadn't drunk so much beer, because the anger is raging inside of me, and I want to just let rip, to incinerate everyone in this shit-hole town, just burn it all fucking down so that I can feel better.

'What's going to happen is that I'm going to leave, get in my stolen car, and drive away, and you are going to go back to whatever depot you're from and tell your superiors that I gave you the slip. Then, you'll never hear from me ever again.'

He swallows. 'What about the next time you decide to...dispense justice?'

He's brave, I'll give him that. And he has a point. But I have no response to this. He can't tell me what to do.

Fuck him.

Fuck them all.

'I'm going now,' I say, making as if to leave, and that's when the waitress hits me from behind with something large and heavy and metal. It makes a loud 'thunk' as it connects with the back of my hairless skull. The blow should knock me out, but it doesn't. I could have told her that, saved her the trouble.

I turn, a playful smile on my lips. She is holding a fire extinguisher out towards me like a talisman, as if I'm an evil spirit to be warded off.

I can feel the fire spreading up my arms now.

'Now that wasn't very friendly, was it?' I purr, rolling my head around on my neck to work out the crick she'd just bashed into it with the extinguisher.

'Get out of my bar, you fucking freak,' she snarls, her mean jowls wobbling with emotion, and I wonder at all these women who seem hate me so, hate me for being just a bit different.

She pulls the pin and sprays foam at me, foam which hisses impotently and then evaporates the second it hits my body.

I grow hotter still with fury, and a steady white glow begins to pulse around me.

How *dare* she?

Can't people just fucking let me be?

Officer Bright is trying to mediate the situation. He does this by pulling his service revolver out and pointing it at me.

'Get on the floor, miss!' He says, his voice shaking. I look back at him over my shoulder.

'How many times do I have to say it? No.'

'Please,' he asks, more gently, and again, I could almost feel some degree of sympathy for him if he weren't pointing a revolver at me.

'Please, I can tell you're angry. I don't want to shoot you. There are good people in this town.'

'I'm leaving now,' I say, and in the distance I hear a train approaching, a freight train, probably. It rattles towards Glenns Ferry at one hell of a speed.

'Ruby Miller! Stop!' Officer Bright shouts after me.

I grow hotter still, and the waitress drops the extinguisher, holding up her arms to protect her face. The approaching freight train sounds its horn: it has no intention of stopping in this shit-hole town. It's going to shoot straight on through, which is what I should have done.

The horn sounds again, closer, and I push open the cafe's door. Officer Bright fires three rounds off in quick succession. They hit me square in the back of the head.

He's a crack shot.

Time slows.

The furnace inside of me boils over. I throw back my head and howl.

Then, I let the fire come.

It washes through the crappy, greasy, go-nowhere bar in the crappy, dusty go-nowhere town like a tidal wave, destroying everything and everyone in its path. I don't stand around watching the wood burn, the tiles blacken, the linoleum blister, the light bulbs explode. I don't look back as the people burn and collapse to the floor in a heap of ash, small piles of teeth scattering about like macabre confetti. I do wonder idly instead why teeth don't seem to burn like the rest of the body.

I walk within the fire, and I leave hell in my wake. Before me, the train approaches, roaring along its track like a great ravenous beast, eating up the miles, dragging containers and tanks behind it, maybe thirty, forty pieces of cargo. The level crossing barriers come down, signalling the approach of the train, and the alarm starts to ding.

An idea hits me, and I act upon it, walking right up the barrier, turning it to cinders with a mere touch. I am on the level crossing now, a blighted, burning torch, a beacon of years of abuse and pain at the hands of my Daddy, my precious Daddy who said he would never hurt me, but he did, people lie, and they deceive, and they manipulate, and they take.

Well now, it is my turn.

I hear shouting behind me, and screaming, as the fire spreads from the cafe to the neighbouring timber buildings on the street. A fire engine blares out in the distance, but it is faint, it is no match for the sound of the blaze and the approaching engine on the tracks.

There is movement, and a rush of electricity along the tracks under my feet. I summon up the last of my grief and my anger and I push it all into the flames, which tower ten feet or so above me. I register dimly the noise of brakes squealing against the train tracks, but the driver has seen me too late, everything is always too little, too late.

As the train thunders towards me I see a warning logo painted onto one of the tankards behind the engine. It's the symbol for a toxic substance, a liquid chemical of some sort, and next to it, a simple, stylized flame, meaning one thing: flammable materials.

The train smacks into me at fifty miles per hour, and the engine up front cleaves clean in two, a great squealing of metal and broken things trumpeting its death.

The tankard follows.

I embrace it.

The resulting explosion, or series of explosions, as the tanks behind the first one go off in succession, like a chain of dominos- well. It is the most glorious thing I have ever seen or heard. The very earth shakes. Huge waves of impact roll outwards from the epicentre of my once-again naked body. Buildings fall. Trees catch fire. Cars flip and tumble over and over down the streets.

People die by the hundreds.

They deserve it, each one of them.

I am the fucking apocalypse.

My name is Ruby Miller.

And I am a Phoenix from the ashes.

I WANDER through the blackened scar I have left on the land, and hear the distant sound of helicopters and law enforcement approaching. I hit the outskirts of town, and find a single street where the fire did not get everything, for some reason. A small pocket of peace in the maelstrom. As I walk down it, I see why.

I see providence.

I see the Gods smiling down at me.

At the end of the half-ruined street, three cars are parked on the sidewalk, still undamaged. The third of these cars is a rare car. You don't find many of them, anymore.

It's a cherry red 1989 Pontiac Bonneville.

I smile.

Time to hit the road.

HELEN

Thank you for coming, Mrs. Miller, I wasn't sure you would. I do appreciate it. Please, come in. Excuse the mess, I've had a hell of a week what with...well, we'll get to that in a moment.

Coffee? I know it's late, but I always keep a pot ready. I don't sleep so well, these days, you see, and I find I need something to keep me going, particularly round about now, mid-afternoon, before my second wind kicks in. I have so much work to do, always so much work, I can't afford to stop, take a break.

Because there are so many things I don't know, yet. *So* many.

Just like there are a great deal of things I wish I *didn't* know. Beautiful, strange, terrifying things. Things that don't make sense, in this world, or at least, the world you and I grew up in.

That world, I am beginning to realise, was a fantasy. The current world is a place of greater intrigue and mystery than you could ever imagine, and what's more, it is weak, worn through in places, *thinner*, if that makes any sense. It doesn't, but it will, in time. It won't be an easy adjustment to make, but over the years, I found I have acclimated to my new reality. It was a painful process, but I have, at last, come to terms with it, come to terms with the weird shit that goes on out there in broad daylight, right under our noses, often without the wider public realising. I mean sure, there are eye witnesses, a few, but we manage that. As much as we can. Sometimes, that is not as easy as I would like, particularly when it comes to your…hmmm.

I'm getting ahead of myself, aren't I? Patience is a virtue, they say, but I've never subscribed to that. Still, everything needs to come in order, or it won't make sense to you. What I'm trying to say is that there are things that…well, it just means I don't sleep very well, like I told you. You can probably tell from the bags under my eyes. *Big enough to pack a swimsuit in*, my husband says.

Oh, boy. You don't have a clue what I am talking about, do you? You have no idea why you are here. That's okay. It's probably easier for me to show you than to stand around talking at you for the next hour. So let's go into my office, shall we? Follow me, Mrs. Miller, if you will, and like I said- excuse the mess.

Okay, here we are. My office. Big, isn't it? It needs to be. I need the wallspace. I need room to walk around, I think best when I'm moving about. Can't be one of those people who sits on their ass all day long, it makes me miserable. I have to be in motion, constant motion. My husband has a hard time with that, which is why I am down here. No one can hear me pacing around, down here. And being underground has…benefits. Benefits that will become evident the more our relationship develops.

So, without further ado, let me ask you a question, a very important question, and your answer will dictate how we move forward from here. Because some people…well, they are simply more…open-minded than others, shall we say.

Ready? Don't look so nervous, there really isn't anything to worry about. I'm just about to open your eyes a little, that's all. What you're about to learn is privileged information. I'm just trying to establish what flavour coating with which to sugar the pill.

Ahem. So, how should I phrase this…ah…oh, for heaven's sake. I'll just come out with it.

Do you believe in monsters, Mrs. Miller?

I can see you're confused by the question, so let me clarify: I don't mean murderers and rapists and child-abusers and social media moguls and politicians and dictators, not that kind of monster. Human monsters. Flesh and blood, like you and me.

No.

I'm talking about *real* monsters. Sasquatch. Werewolves. The Boogeyman. Vampires. Giants. Wendigos. That kind of shit.

I can see by your face that your answer is a big, fat, resounding, no.

That's fine. I was the same, once. No, I'm not laughing at you, please don't think that. I'm just…well, humour is how I cope with all this, you see. Gallows-humour, I think they call it. Making light of something dark.

Because you see, Mrs. Miller, whether or not you believe in them, monsters are, undeniably, irrefutably, inconveniently, very, very real indeed.

I can see you nervously eyeing the door, wondering how to get out of this situation. I can assure you that I am not insane, remarkable really, considering the things I've seen, but, part of this job involves me having regular assessments by psychiatrists and other mental health specialists, and unfortunately for you, I am perfectly okay 'upstairs'. I am also not a liar, nor a fabulist, which leaves only one option for you: to accept that I am telling the truth. The world is chock-full to the brim of supernatural shit, right now, shit that doesn't make any sense at all by the rules against which we as a species have propped ourselves up for all these thousands of years. But those rules no longer apply, Mrs. Miller. We have an outbreak on our hands. A plague, if you like, of unexplainable phenomena.

And you have a part to play in helping us to fight this plague.

Don't believe me? Take a look. These walls are covered in proof, and there is more in those filing cabinets over there, and far more besides. Photographs, video stills, eyewitness accounts, censored social media posts, audio samples, newspaper clippings, redacted police reports, forensics, I have it all. Mulder and Scully would cream their pants twice over if they saw this office. I shouldn't really be showing you all this, but what the hell. The older I get, the more complacent I become, because soon, none of this will be here anyway. Not unless we can get a handle on the new state of play.

Don't be afraid, you can take a closer look. I trust you. Why? For the simple reason that even if you do tell others what you've seen within these walls, nobody out there is going to believe you. They're all like you. Sceptical. That's how humans are raised, these days.

Just look at the pictures, you'll see what I mean. Oh, and before you cry *'fake!'* *'These are all fake!'*, I have other proof. Physical, living proof. I just think, at this stage, you might be a little too delicate for me to expose you to it. So why don't you browse the walls, instead? Start off gentle.

I wish someone had started *me* off gentle.

Are you beginning to understand, now? I can see from your face that maybe you are. It's a lot to take in, isn't it?

So many strange things that just simply shouldn't exist. I call them 'Anomalies.' Others would call them proof of the supernatural, maybe evidence of God, or magic, or evil, or the devil. I don't like any of those descriptions, but I do like 'Anomaly', because that is what these things are. Something that deviates from the normal. Something that is unexpected.

Take that picture, for example. Yeah, that's its location, pinpointed on the British Ordinance Survey map next to it. Looks like a field full of cows, doesn't it? Harmless enough. Now look at this photo. Same cows. Spot the difference, up close? See the teeth? Sharp, and pointed, instead of flat and square? See the subtle difference in bone structure around the jaw, the variations in hoof size?

See the bones in the field, hiding amongst the grass?

Yeah. Those cows don't eat grass.

They eat flesh.

Or at least they did, until we exterminated the herd. Well, *almost* all the herd. We kept two alive, for study. Sound drastic? Maybe, but our actions were not without good reason. And our Zoology department is having a field day, if you'll pardon the expression, trying to figure out the biological composition of these things. They certainly aren't bovine, not any more. If you look over there, on my desk, you'll see a small glass case filled with the Bull's front canines. Not something I ever thought I'd hear myself saying. Take a closer look. They look like vampire teeth, don't they? Perfectly evolved to puncture flesh. Hollow in the centre, too, for what reason, we can't determine. Snakes have hollow teeth to deliver venom, but we've found no evidence of poison sacs or the like, not yet, at any rate. Still, pretty fucked up, right?

This is what I mean by 'Anomaly'.

Oh, that one? That's the Norfolk Manor police report,

obviously heavily redacted. It's not there anymore, the manor house, which is a shame, really. The property was bulldozed a few years back, but not before I managed to get a team out there to collect samples. Yes, you're completely correct- that is indeed a human eye growing in the middle of that flower upon that vine. We took cuttings, and we have an extremely patient horticulturist working on trying to get them to take root. Again, for study, you understand. The more we learn, the more we can anticipate and fight back. Because these things were kind of prolific, the entire estate was covered in those vines, smothered almost completely. Extraordinary, right? Rather beautiful, too. Complete assimilation by a plant of a human being. The vine network redistributed the human parts across the estate over a number of years, and honestly, if I weren't so busy, I would dedicate *all* of my time to this one case. It haunts me. It fascinates me. The blend of botanical and human. I still have a hard time dealing with it, honestly. I dream of that eye, a lot.

Ah, that one's harder to explain. The stream. Again, in Britain. In fact, the whole island seems to be something of a hotspot for Anomalies, why, we're not sure. And don't even get me started on Scotland. I may have to move there soon, if things continue the way they are. Anyway, looks harmless enough, doesn't it? Unless you drink from it. Infested, in a uniquely localised way, you see, with what I can only describe as 'wigglers.' A parasite, of sorts. See that microscope over there? I've got a few on a plate for you to look at, if you fancy. No? Not your thing? Fair enough. I wouldn't get too close, anyway, contact with the wigglers only has one result, as far as we can see: skin irritation to the point where those afflicted rip their own dermis off, in long, tortured strips. I've seen it with my own eyes. I lost quite a bit of weight, after that one. I didn't eat or drink anything properly for weeks. Infections and parasites are really not my thing either, you see.

Ah, that's a sad one. Rat Boy. Poor thing, he has no memory of what his life was like before he was bitten. Don't let the ears and tail deceive you- he might look cute, but he's wild, completely wild. Rats are intelligent, you see, enormously so. Survivalists. There was another one, before him, a girl. The one that bit him, turned him. She escaped, which was an unfortunate oversight, one I won't let happen again. We have this one under tight observation, now, although what we'll do with him once he outgrows his cell, I don't know.

I can see you need a break. Why don't you come and sit down, over here, I'll pour you a drink. Are you a scotch person? Single malt? Gin? Vodka? I have poison to suit all tastes.

Scotch it is, good choice. Here we go. I think I'll have one too, it's been a long day already.

Me? That's a good question, I thought you'd never ask. Well, I *used* to be a behavioral analyst and profiler for the FBI, but then, one Christmas, that changed. It changed in the most brutal and unexpected of ways, and I, through stint of being in the wrong place at the wrong time, ended up with a promotion. Sorry, I should stop being so vague, shouldn't I? Habit, I'm afraid, but I don't need to hide anything from you, and it is an interesting story. You see, I was called in to help with a series of nasty murders, murders which all took place on Christmas morning. The thinking at the time was that there was a serial killer at work, one who was drawn to the Nativity, for some fucked-up reason of his own, but oh, how wrong we were. It wasn't a serial killer, not even close. It was a predator, a creature unlike anything I have ever seen before. Don't ask me to describe it, I can't. There is a photograph over there, next to the picture of that strange Jack-in-the-box, which, by the way, I wouldn't look at too closely, not if you're the squeamish type. There, that one. Yeah, it's dead now, but see what I mean? Imagine *that* crawling down your chimney. There's a little girl out there who doesn't have to imagine, who will probably never celebrate Christmas again, I can tell you that. I send her a card each year, and a gift, but I think she'd rather I didn't. I think she'd rather forget all about me, and I can't say I blame her.

My new job title? I can't tell you what my new job title is, exactly, because it's a secret, although I don't mind telling you that I've not really looked back since I got promoted. I don't miss my old work. I got tired, you see, of learning about the bad things men and women do to each other. It was easier, somehow, to come to terms with the bad things Anomalies do, because it feels more like...nature, I guess. The Anomalies don't really understand the concept of right, or wrong. They don't seem to have a moral compass, or lack thereof. They simply exist. They are not motivated, or driven, not in a psychological sense. You can't, therefore, predict them, at least, not yet. They are events out of our control. My job is to pick up the pieces *after* these events happen, and develop an understanding of how each Anomaly relates to the other. Look for patterns, that kind of thing. Because they are related, they are linked, I know that now. The world is thin in places, like I said, and wherever that thinness manifests, strange things happen. I mentioned Scotland before. There is a tiny little Island in the northern Highlands that had a giant, can you believe that? A whole town disappeared without a trace up there, and they had a *giant*. The thinness in that place was the most concentrated I'd ever seen, until…

Well, until we found the Arch.

But I'm getting off track. There's another reason I brought you here, and it isn't to talk about that, although I would say, as a precaution, maybe you should consider investing in a storm shelter or bunker of some sort, going forward, something underground. Once we're done with you, that is. Stockpile some canned goods. I don't mean to alarm you, but it can't hurt to be prepared, can it?

Now then, we can finally get down to the brass nuts and bolts of why you're here. I won't beat around the bush anymore, Mrs. Miller, I have done enough of that today. You are here because I am in the business of tracking Anomalies, as I have said, tracking them and cleaning up after them.

And it has come to my attention, in the last few weeks, that a new Anomaly has come to town. That Anomaly has a name, Mrs. Miller, and her name is Ruby.

Yes, that's right, your daughter Ruby.

I'm afraid she's been doing some rather dreadful things, lately, and I don't just mean the alleged murder of your husband. Things that have required...a lot of cleaning up. I could show you some distressing drone footage we have of an unfortunate place called Glenns Ferry, which by now you've probably heard of, but I am not sure how helpful that would be. And no, it wasn't a chemical explosion, or at least, not in the way the media is reporting it. It was a *Ruby* explosion, a signature move, and what frightens me, almost as much as the Arch I mentioned earlier, is that I think your girl is...

Well, to be frank, I think she is just getting started.

And this is where I must also contradict myself, somewhat, because Ruby is undoubtedly an Anomaly, true. But, unlike all the others I have dealt with thus far, Ruby *is* motivated by human desires, and feelings, and urges, and her own, somewhat warped sense of morality, payback, duty, whatever. And that makes her dangerous, Mrs. Miller, really, really dangerous. In my old job, I would have had to label her a 'spree killer,' typified as someone who kills on a whim, someone driven by impulsive urges, someone damaged and wounded and vengeful, looking to maximise the pain of others as a way out of her own pain.

You had no idea? Well that much is obvious. I try not to judge, Mrs. Miller, but I don't think you will be winning any parenting awards any time soon, no offence intended.

Where do you fit into all this?

So, and I must apologise for repeating myself so often and in such a circular fashion, but the more I know and understand about an Anomaly, the more I can fight back against the chaos they spread.

And more the point, I *need* Ruby. I don't just want to curb her behaviour, although if someone doesn't soon, there won't be much of a planet worth saving, I'm sure. But beyond her acting out, I need her.

For a...task.

But we're having a hard time figuring out how to get her on our side, Mrs. Miller, and *that* is where you come in.

Oh, these guys? They work for me, don't worry. Snuck up on you without warning, didn't they? Ha ha, it helps that I drugged your drink, sorry about that. It's not personal, I assure you. I just can't take any chances at the moment. Now, try not to struggle too much when they...I said *don't* struggle, Mrs. Miller, you'll only make those zip-ties tighter! I wish people would listen to me, I really do. And I really wouldn't bother wasting energy on screams, nobody can hear you down here, like I said before. My office is underground for a reason.

Oh well, in a moment you won't have the strength to scream, anyway, not when those drugs really kick in.

I do very much appreciate your cooperation, Mrs.

Miller, I hope you know that. And rest assured, I won't be needing your help for long, just long enough time to...persuade Ruby to listen to me.

Oh, and in case I forget, I'm not entirely sure I introduced myself properly, earlier. It's probably a good idea for us to be on more familiar terms, particularly as you'll be staying here for a little while. I know your name, but I don't think you know mine.

My name is Helen. For the purposes of this job, I have no last no last name. Helen will be enough, for you.

Helen.

It's a name your daughter is about to get very familiar with.

CAT

4

I keep telling you, I don't *know* Ruby Miller!

Not like you think I do!

I just happened to be in the wrong place at the wrong time, I didn't even know she fucking existed half an hour before you showed up!

Why won't you believe me?!

Who even *are* you fucking people? And what the fuck is this place, some sort of underground bunker? What, are you survivalist freaks? You're not government, you don't look like government, anyway, even if you are packing enough equipment to arm a small country.

Whatever, I don't care, the point is, you know you've kidnapped me, right? You know you're holding me against my will? You know I have rights, don't you? You can't just throw people into unmarked vans and interrogate them, this is America! *Fuck!*

Just...can't I even have a little water? It's been...hours...and my head…

But I already *told* you everything I know! Why the fuck aren't you listening to me?

Oh, once more, for the tape? Is that it?

What happened to the first three fucking tapes?! Fuck you, let me out of here! Untie my fucking hands, and let me...

Wait.

Wait!

You don't need to use that.

Seriously, get that fucking thing away from me, I swear to god, you're making me beg like a fucking animal, and I can't tell you any more than I already *have*, you can do whatever you fucking like to me, do whatever you want to my body, and it won't change the story, because I am telling you the fucking truth, okay?!

Okay.

Please, don't! I can't...please, you don't need that, okay?!

I SAID GET THAT FUCKING THING AWAY FROM ME!

Jesus. Jesus Christ, that hurt, that hurt so much, I...please, stop, I'll talk!

I'll talk.

Once more then, for the fucking tape, you animals.

But not without water.

Water first, and then I talk.

And take that fucking thing out of the room with you, I won't say another word until it's out of sight, you fucking sadists, do you hear me?

Good.

Thank you. At last, someone is *listening* to me.

Alright, give me a motherfucking moment, you monster, I've been here hours without so much as a sip of water and...oh, God, that feels good. *So* good. Fuck, damn, I never want to...just a bit more, I'm not done yet, I need more...fine.

I'm ready, I'll talk. You don't need to...good. But...just stand over there, would you? Over by that wall. I don't fucking trust you, not one bit, you vicious piece of...

Okay, okay, fine. I will tell you everything I know about Ruby Miller.

And after, you're going to let me go, right?

Right?

5

I first met Ruby Miller sitting in a diner. She was alone, and looked raw about it. I noticed her because she was tall, and terrifying. She stared bitterly into the distance at nothing in particular, tapping a single fingernail against an empty soda bottle that was one of many lined up on the counter next to her. She drank as if she had just crawled out of the desert, as if she hadn't drunk in years, desperately finishing each bottle off in a single thirsty effort, before smacking it down and ordering the next.

I was instantly drawn to Ruby. She was unlike anyone I had ever set eyes upon before. Before she'd walked into Petey's Diner I had seen, through the window, a cherry-red Pontiac Bonneville draw up outside and glide into a space in the half-empty parking lot. That car raised more than a few eyebrows. Folk in these parts don't drive vintage cars. They drive practical cars, pickups and muscular gas-guzzlers with plenty of space in the back in which to throw something dead during hunting season. Pontiacs are not practical cars. Ruby's Bonneville stood out in the parking lot every bit as much as she did herself in Petey's Diner. Like a sore thumb.

The headlights switched off, and I watched as a long, strong pair of legs exited the car feet-first, followed by a young woman who was easily the tallest I have ever seen. She crossed the parking lot and strode into Petey's as if she owned the place, ignoring everyone as she slammed herself down into a seat.

Two teenage girls on the table next to me giggled behind their menus.

'Check out the edge-queen,' one of them said, rolling her eyes.

'I thought that whole angry-murder goth thing died out like, twenty years ago,' the other one replied, smirking.

'She's just trying to make up for having small tits,' the first said, looking pleased with herself. They both sat up straighter then, pushing their chests out and preening themselves, using the glassy screens of their smartphones for mirrors, reapplying lip gloss and silently congratulating each other on how hot they looked. Then they snapped a selfie together, heads artfully angled to make them look skinnier than they were, and I shook my head, flicking a look at the newcomer to see if she'd heard any of this exchange.

If she had, she chose to ignore it. She kept her head turned and her eyes forward, which suited me just fine, because it meant I could look at her without interruption. I knew I wasn't the only one doing the same thing. Ruby was hard not to look at. A muted quiet came over the diner as people acclimated to the newcomer.

It wasn't just Ruby's height that made her stand out, or her looks, or her attitude. It was her head, shaved down to a fine sheen of stubble, her bare scalp exaggerating her physique and making her look somehow vulnerable and hard-bitten at the same time. Girls in these parts don't shave their heads. Girls in these parts look like the girls on the table next to me, homogeneous and wholesome. Being 'alternative' is not encouraged. I should know, I've tried a few times. My desire to be different was knocked out of me pretty quick by my parents, and I'm ashamed to say I gave in pretty quick, too, anything for an easier life. Now, I look like most of the other girls from around there- small, petite, my blonde hair drawn into a ponytail that is both practical and, apparently, 'cute'.

Nothing like Ruby.

And I just couldn't keep my eyes off her. She sat so still and calm she looked almost unreal, as if she'd been carved out of marble and placed at the diner bar in a strategic spot like an art installation.

But it was the tattoo I loved the most.

On the back of Ruby's head, embracing the round curve of her flawless skull, was a delicate line tattoo of a bird: a phoenix, wings outspread, tail curling down the nape of Ruby's neck. I wondered what it would be like to run a finger along and around the thin black contours of that tattoo. I wondered what it would be like to hold that head in my hands, lay a kiss on those lips.

In short, Ruby was too good an opportunity to miss.

She lit a fire under my ass.

Feeling braver than I'd ever felt before in my life, I pushed away from my usual table against the wall, in the corner of the room, and took a seat next to her at the bar. Ruby ignored me as I sat down, still staring into space. She looked like she had a lot going on in that head of hers, like she had a lot of memories to sort through, and they were heavy ones at that. I cleared my throat, offered to buy her a soda. My words, delivered quietly, fell on deaf ears. I repeated myself, louder this time.

'I said, would you like another soda? On me? You look thirsty.'

Raphael, the owner, and also my landlord, gave us both the side-eye from behind the bar as I repeated my question. He shook his head minutely, a gesture that I ignored, because I knew what it meant: *Don't bring any of that queer stuff into my diner*, it meant. *This is not the place for it. In this diner, men date women and women date men, just as God intended.* Usually, again, for a quiet life, I respected that rule. Raphael was not a bad man, or a bigoted one, just a man trying to run a successful business in a one-trade town where the wrong kind of gossip could end a person's livelihood in a matter of days. He should know, he had inherited his business from his Uncle Petey, who was now serving time for fraud and money laundering. Why he didn't change the name away from 'Petey's Diner', I could never understand. Regardless, he was a popular man and a good landlord, and didn't mind if I was late on rent or smoked a joint or two on a Sunday afternoon.

Still. Ruby was the first woman I had ever seen where trying was worth more than the grief I'd get afterwards for doing so.

The trying didn't seem to be paying off, though, because my second offer still didn't get a response. Ruby carried on ignoring me, and I took this as a challenge, feeling my blood more than I'd ever felt it before. I ruminated for a moment, popped my bubble gum, and winked at Raphael. He sighed, shook his head in disapproval, collected two root beers from a fridge, and set them down in front of me. I slid one slowly across the counter and in front of the woman who cold-shouldered me, then sat, waiting, quietly sipping my own drink and wondering what would happen next.

Eventually, Ruby turned and half-looked at me. Her

eyes were like nothing I'd ever seen before: they shone amber and gold in the overheads, almost fire-bright. My breath caught in my throat.

'I didn't say yes,' she said, sullenly, and I realised from her voice that she was younger than I'd originally thought.

I blinked, swallowed, then shrugged. 'You didn't say no, either,' I replied, and there was a slight spark of something in Ruby's eyes in response to this.

I took this as encouragement.

'I'm Cat,' I said, holding out a hand. Ruby stared at it for a moment.

'You shouldn't be talking to me,' she said, and her voice was heavy, flat. 'I'm not a very nice person.'

I blinked. 'How do you know that *I* am?' I kept my hand where it was: outstretched, waiting.

Ruby snorted, and reluctantly returned the gesture. Her fingers were long, slender, dry, and very, *very* hot. I almost snatched my own fingers out of her grasp, wincing. I wondered if she was running a fever, she was so warm, but everything else about her seemed normal, healthy. In fact, the more I looked, the more I could see she was a complete picture of health: clear skin, alert, bright eyes, strong, upright posture, white, straight teeth. The more I looked, the more I felt ugly, small, diminutive. I began to realise, with a sinking feeling, that I was punching way above my weight. I thought momentarily about backing out, about making a hasty apology and leaving, but I was committed now, and the longer I sat there, the more capti-vated I was.

'I'm Ruby,' said Ruby, and we sized each other up, my initial bravado dwindling the longer I sat baking in the fierce glow that she threw out. It wasn't just how physically prepossessing she was. Ruby gave off an aura of something I had never seen before: raw confidence, and power.

Underneath that, something darker, something else I couldn't put a finger on, exactly. She languidly lifted her root beer to her lips, and drank thirstily from the bottle in such a way that I had to lower my eyes, so that Ruby wouldn't see what she was doing to me.

'So, Cat,' Ruby said eventually, not relaxing her rigid posture.

'So,' I said, awkwardly.

'What do you do around here?'

'For work?' *Oh, boy*, I thought. *She had to ask me that.*

Ruby laughed, dry, humourless. 'Yeah, for work.'

I took a deep breath. 'Well, I work where everyone else around here works, in the Resource Recovery Facility on Route One North.'

'Recovery Facility?'

'I can tell you're new in town.' I shook my head. Raphael chuckled to himself, shamelessly eavesdropping on us while he polished glasses with a dish towel.

'It's a giant trash incinerator,' I continued, embarrassed.

Ruby's head came up from her beer.

'Incinerator?' She said, her interest clearly piqued, but before she could continue, a purple-haired, leather-clad woman seemingly materialised out of thin air from behind us, screamed in fury, swung her arm down hard, and stuck a giant carving knife into the back of Ruby's head.

6

I reared back, horrified, almost falling off my seat, feeling drops of blood land on my face as the women yanked the knife out. She stabbed down again, and I heard the noise of the blade grinding past bone and flesh clearly, saw the knife sink deep into Ruby's skull.

Thunk! It went.

The noise was awful, meaty and metallic at the same time, and I covered my mouth in terror and shock.

'*Bitch!*' The woman screamed, and she yanked the knife free with effort, jiggling the blade to release it from where it was lodged. Another spray of blood flew through the air, and the woman swung down again, and again, and again. Ruby fell to the floor, her long body crashing down heavily, and the purple-haired woman crowed in triumph, waving the massive knife around like a flag on parade day. Then she lifted her arm one last time, and slammed the blade deep into the back of Ruby's skull, right in the very middle of that phoenix tattoo I loved so much.

I heard myself screaming as I looked at the handle sticking out proud, the blade buried in the young woman's brain, right up to the hilt. Behind me, other people were screaming too, chairs scraping back, cellphones coming out to film what was happening. I heard some people leave, heard car engines fire up. I heard others swear and curse, rooted to the spot like I was, staring at the bloody mess of a woman on the floor.

Something bright flickered for a moment as I looked at her still body, something white and nebulous, but it was gone in an instant.

What the fuck?! I thought, frantically, over and over, *What the fuck?!*

A mountainous figure lumbered into view: Jordan, one of the chefs at Petey's Diner. Jordan was supposed to be off-shift, but everyone who was off-shift hung out in Petey's anyway, and this was why: they might miss something if they didn't. Jordan was big, massive, and the crazy woman with purple hair was not. He came up behind her and wrapped her up tight in a bear hug, his face grim and implacable. She squealed and fought, but she may as well have been fighting against a mountain. Jordan hung on, and Raphael scrambled for the phone hanging behind the bar, intent on dialling 911. He clawed it off the hook, and was just about to dial when a woman's voice cut strong and clear over the chaos.

'*Wait!*' It said.

Raphael's finger paused, hovering over his phone's keypad.

My eyes travelled to the girl on the floor, the girl with a six inch knife blade jammed hard into her skull.

The girl who should be dead.

Only, Ruby wasn't dead.

She pushed up from the ground, frowning as she looked down at her own blood pooling around her.

'Goddammit, Violet,' she complained, glaring at the

purple-haired woman who had gone limp for a moment in Jordan's arms. 'You made a real mess this time, didn't you? Crazy bitch.'

Then, she stood up, holding out a hand to Raphael in a staying motion: *no police,* it said.

Those of us left in the diner gasped.

'Don't call anyone,' Ruby said, calmly. 'I don't need the cops in here, poking their noses into my business.'

Raphael stared at Ruby, his face white. He saw what I saw, what we all saw: the knife handle sticking right out of the back of her head. She wore it like an accessory, even though the blade was, at this very moment, slicing through her brain, wedged in so far and hard it was a wonder the knife tip didn't poke out of her left nostril for the world to see.

'Honey,' Raphel said, eventually, his voice shaking as he tried to remain calm. 'You might not want the cops, but you sure as shit need an ambulance.'

Ruby smiled.

'Oh, you mean this?' She said, and reached behind herself slowly, grasping the knife handle. There was a sick, wet grinding noise, the noise of metal on bone, like a knife being sharpened slowly, only it was worse than that, grittier and wetter and more ominous, and then, with a little effort, she pulled the crimson blade out, and threw it to the floor. It clanged down into a stunned silence, splattering more of Ruby's bright red blood across the linoleum.

The woman with purple hair howled in rage.

'Why won't you fucking *die?!*' She screamed, and Ruby kept on smiling.

I almost, but not quite, fainted.

7

'Violet, Violet, Violet,' Ruby said, tutting and cocking her head to one side and rubbing the back of her head absently. There should have been a wound where she was rubbing, there should have been blood and bone and brains, but instead, there was only skin, lightly stubbled, with a tattoo running unblemished across her scalp. I felt light-headed, and queasy. What was going on here? What had I just seen?

I wasn't the only one struggling. You could hear a pin drop in the diner as we all watched what was unfolding with disbelief.

Ruby moved closer to her attacker. Her voice dripped with false camaraderie.

'Hey, V. It's been a while, hasn't it. Are you still following me around? Really?'

Violet snarled and lunged at Ruby, hands clawed, reaching for her eyes. Whoever this woman was, she had long since lost grip on her sanity. She was wild, like an animal, and had only one thing in mind: getting Ruby. Jordan's grip on her stayed firm, largely because he was so shocked he didn't know what else to do. He just hung on, for dear life. Violet howled in frustration, scratching and clawing at the arms that held her in place.

Ruby shook her head, looking tired.

'You can't keep doing this to yourself, Violet. Look at you. You're killing yourself. I've driven dozens of miles, ended up in dozens of towns and you've been in every single one, two steps behind me, the whole way. Aren't you tired, honey? Don't you want to go home?'

Violet arched her back and tried to reach Ruby with her booted feet, flailing about as if she were possessed. I saw tattoos on Violet's legs, symbols that I recognised from TV shows and newspaper articles. Gang symbols. Biker gang symbols, to be specific.

Ruby watched as Violet thrashed around and wore herself slowly down, Jordan still clinging to her like a limpet. She tutted.

'I knew I made a mistake, letting you live. You're a zealot, Violet. Found yourself any new rapist friends lately?'

Violet stopped struggling, temporarily exhausted, and hung trembling in Jordan's embrace, panting, covered in sweat. Her shoulders heaved, and she spat.

Ruby watched her, that small, cold smile still on her lips.

'I'll take that as a no,' she said, dryly.

'You killed them, you fucking freak!' Violet yelled, the first coherent words I'd heard from her mouth. Her lower lip wobbled with fear and hate. 'You killed my boys!'

This was a new twist.

I watched Ruby, who seemed unshaken, accommodating almost, like she was used to Violet's histrionics. I still couldn't see a single scratch on Ruby's head, and it bothered me, it bothered me more than anything else. I couldn't stop staring at her perfect, unbroken skin.

Because there should have been a wound.

Because, in truth, there should have been a body lying on the floor.

Violet hawked another gobbet of phlegm into her mouth and projected it full into Ruby's face. The ball of spit hit the other woman on the bridge of her nose, and Ruby flinched involuntarily, closed her eyes in disgust, then laughed, throaty and deep. Again, there was a tiny glimmer of light, an outline of something brilliant that flared and then disappeared and left me blinking, with tiny bright spots in my eyes. My senses alive, that curious light feeling growing stronger in me by the moment, I heard something, then. A faint sizzling sound, barely audible over the noise of Violet swearing as she saw her missile hit home.

But I heard it.

And seconds later, the trembling white gobbet of spit on Ruby's handsome face had gone, seemingly evaporated into thin air, and my mouth dropped open.

What the fuck?! I thought, my skin tingling.

Did I just see that?

I remembered Ruby's hot, hot fingers, when she'd taken my hand.

Did that...did I really just see that?

Something is...what is this?

I felt lighter still, as if I were about to float off the floor and bump into the ceiling.

Something is wrong here!

Ruby rolled her head around on her neck, as if working out a kink, flexed her shoulders, cracked her knuckles theatrically, and held up both hands in front of Violet's face. Violet shrank back in terror, eyes wide and red-rimmed, as if she knew something the rest of us didn't.

Ruby's hands exploded into twin bouquets of blinding white fire.

THE ENTIRE DINER surged out of their seats and scrambled back in terror. I sagged at the knees and fell back against the bar, shaking, mesmerised by the flames that licked and curled from Ruby's fingers.

'I don't want to be followed anymore, Violet,' Ruby said, patiently, as if talking to a very small child, and the fire grew brighter, too bright to look at. I flung my hands over my eyes. I didn't want to see this. This couldn't be happening. This was insane. It was too much. It was all too much.

Ruby's voice continued, as if nothing out of the ordinary were happening at all.

'I know you're pissed, Violet, I get it. You're hurting, and you want revenge. I know how that feels. More than anyone, trust me. I killed your boys, didn't I? Your crew. Never mind that I was naked and lost and needed help and they tried to...well, you know what they tried to do to me. You were there, weren't you? And you did jack shit about it. But no, no, of course, *I'm* the one in the wrong.'

Violet made ugly animal noises. Despite my better judgement, I peeked at her through my fingers, and saw that all sense and reason had gone from the woman's face.

'You deserve to die, you fucking freak!' she yelled, her eyes wide and deranged in the glare of the fire. 'I'm not afraid of you! I'll fucking follow you until I see you dead, I *swear!*'

Ruby closed her eyes, and whispered something that only I was close enough to hear.

'I just wanted a quiet life,' she said to herself, bitterly. 'I just wanted...I just wanted a new start.'

The veins in Violet's neck stood proud as she strained once more towards Ruby.

'You killed my boys and left me out there in that desert to *die,* you cunt! I'm gonna fucking follow you to gates of hell if I have to, you stupid fucking freak *bitch!*'

'Shut up Violet,' said Ruby, in a matter of fact way. 'I'm bored of you, now.'

She spread her hands wide in a sweeping gesture, and the fire lurched forward like a dog let off a leash.

Violet screamed. The unmistakable smell of burning flesh and hair filled the air. Jordan swore, and flung himself backwards. I took my hands from my eyes and clamped them over my nose and mouth, protecting myself from the awful stench. I saw people duck down beneath tables, and run to hide in the washrooms. Raphael and I remained fixed to the spot as the woman with purple hair burst into flames and roasted, right there in front of us.

And I watched, despite myself.

Violet bucked and lurched amidst the flames, screaming, performing a wild, agonised dance before her arms contracted to her chest and her knees buckled beneath her and then, mercifully, because I *just could not look away*, the flames obliterated anything recognisably human.

It was all over in seconds.

The screams cut off, as if someone flicked a switch.

Ruby stood, fire still flowing from her like water, her face set and stony, her head cocked to one side. I realised that she was not new to killing, she had done it before, and would do it again. I knew what I was looking at: anger, fresh and unfettered, and I knew there was an endless well of it inside of her, I just *knew*. All you had to do was take a look at Ruby's face. I felt sick to my stomach as I stared at her.

I then noticed, in a slow, drunken sort of way, as if I'd had twenty beers and not two sodas, that the linoleum floor around my feet was melting, was now sticky, tar-like. I shifted back, and my feet came away with strands of melted lino stuck to the soles. I knew heat and fire, everyone who worked at the incineration plant was familiar with the stuff, but this was something else. This was localised, this was *specific*, somehow. This was fire made into a weapon: deadlier than a gun. This was...

I sobbed, unable to help myself.

This was fucking *elemental*, somehow.

The flames died down, but the smell did not.

God, it was *awful.*

I gagged, and a pile of black, charred matter collapsed softly onto the floor in the exact place a woman in leather called Violet had stood moments earlier.

There was a dead, complete silence.

Ruby sighed, contemplating the charcoaled remains of her assailant, and then turned, taking in the scene as people cowered against the walls and under tables and crowded behind the washroom doors for protection. Their fear seemed to give her a strange type of resolve. Her back straightened, and her shoulders squared. She stared down the bridge of her nose at the entire room, holding eye-contact with each and every person in turn as her gaze swept across us, like a goddamned queen on execution day staring into the eyes of her assembled court, daring them to question her will.

Then, in a sudden, urgent scramble, as if a collective penny had dropped, the patrons of Petey's Bar scattered for freedom, and ran from the building. Except for Raphael, who was trapped behind the bar.

And me.

I had a clear path to the door, and I didn't take it.

I don't know why. I don't know why I didn't run. I could have, but I stayed. I don't think my brain was working properly. I think I was in shock, looking back. Do I regret staying, now? At this precise moment in time, yes. Yes I do. I don't really remember thinking anything, back then. I just stood there, rapt, frozen in place in some kind of dreadful awe, stuck before the most beautiful, terrifying woman I'd ever set eyes upon. A beautiful nightmare.

I realised that Ruby was talking to me.

'I need you to do me a favour,' she said.

I nodded, slowly, unable to speak.

It wasn't exactly like I could say no, now was it?

I could feel sweat building under my armpits, trickling down my sides. Ruby didn't belong to the same world as me, or Raphael. She belonged to a world in which fire and death did as she bid, like a trained pet. My feelings of detachment intensified, and the voice that came out of me didn't sound one bit like my own.

'What do you want?' I said.

But before she could answer, something whizzed past my ear with a high-pitched whistle, hitting Ruby hard on her right shoulder, and sticking there, proud as the knife had stuck out of her head earlier. She frowned, and plucked it out.

It was a tranquilizer dart.

Her eyes widened when she realised what it was.

'Seriously?' she said, exasperated, and was immediately hit with another dart, and then another, and another. Within seconds, a storm of darts hurtled at her from somewhere behind me, dozens of them, coming at her like deadly, sideways rain, and she was suddenly covered, darts sprouting out all over her skin and clothes so she resembled something like a weird, grisly, two-legged porcupine.

She roared, and I snapped into reflex mode, hoisting myself up and over the bar to where Raphael cowered, glasses tumbling down and smashing everywhere, and I tucked my head under my hands, right in close to my chest, my knees drawn up tight against me, cowering, knowing now what was coming next.

The fire surged.

The air over my head crackled and popped.

But the darts kept coming, from where exactly, I couldn't tell, and suddenly, miraculously, there was quiet, and a temperature drop.

The firestorm stopped.

Panting and shaking with fear, I slowly poked my head out from behind the bar, because I had to see. I just had to.

And see I did. I saw Ruby, sinking reluctantly to her knees on the floor. Her face was warped and twisted with fury, fury that melted into a quiet, fuzzy expression of confusion. Her flames guttered and finally winked out. Hundreds of darts covered every inch of her entire body, and she feebly began to pull them out, one by one, but wasn't quick enough. She folded from her knees and smacked down onto the melted linoleum like a felled tree, face turned towards me.

That's when you guys showed up.

A stranger, clad in black, with some sort of military jacket and reflective mask over his face, stepped lightly into the diner. He looked down at the woman lying by his feet, and prodded her with one booted toe. Ruby lay motionless, face still turned to me, dribble leaking out of her mouth and pooling on the floor.

And as I peered at all this across the bar, something was jammed, lightning quick, into my neck.

A tranq dart.

You fucking tranqued me.

Thanks, assholes.

Strong arms held me down, pressed my face into the metal bar-top. I lay still, pinned heavily in place by a person I couldn't see. Whatever was in the dart acted fast. It flowed into my veins and began its work right away. I felt my body relax, noticing, as I went limp, that there were more men in the room. They surrounded Ruby, and seemed to be arranging some sort of gelatinous membrane on the ground, preparing to roll her onto it, I assumed.

One of your men leaned down, a syringe in his hand, intending to inject more stuff into Ruby's long neck. Another sheet of membrane was spread out to one side, and I could see that they meant to make a sticky kind of sealed, air-tight shroud, or pocket around the woman. I wondered sleepily who they were, and what the membrane was made out of, and if it was fireproof, because boy, would Ruby be pissed when she woke up to find herself vacuum-packed like a chicken fillet in a freezer cabinet.

Whoever had pinned me to the bar let go, then, and my limp body began to slide backwards off the bar. I felt my vision blur, and my bladder gave out. Warm liquid slid down my legs.

In the last, final few seconds before I lost consciousness, Ruby's eyes met mine. Heavy boots moved quickly around her, but I got a good, clear look at her face before it all went black.

I thought, with a bleary, weak sort of hope, that her slack mouth might tighten into a predatory smile.

I thought she might wink at me, light up, glow, obliterate the men in black with a signature explosion, but she didn't.

She closed her eyes instead, and I closed mine.

And then, I fucking woke up here.

Tied to a chair, in a dark, cold, windowless room made of concrete, with a whole row of suited assholes staring at me and demanding I tell them everything I know about Ruby Miller.

So, I have.

Can I fucking go now?

RUBY

9

'Hello Ruby,' Daddy said, from the darkness. It was late afternoon, and he was in my bedroom. I was lying on the bed, reading a magazine and listening to music.

'Hey,' I said, unenthusiastically. Daddy had been behaving weird just lately, more weird than normal, and it was starting to make me feel uncomfortable. Even Mom had told me to steer clear of him, although she wouldn't elaborate on why, exactly. I was pretty sure that accounted for all the time she spent out of the house, though. Anyway, I didn't need her advice. I couldn't put my finger on what it was, but I felt like something was not quite right between me and Daddy, and I didn't know what was, or what to do about it, so I took to hiding in my bedroom as much as possible instead.

But now he was here, and he seemed to want something, and I was jiggered if I could figure out what.

I didn't need to figure it out, as it happened.

He was more than happy enough to show me.

'Want to play a special Daddy-Daughter game?' He

said, locking the door behind him and leaning back against it. His face was flushed, his hair dishevelled. He folded his arms, as if hugging himself.

'What?' I said, irritable and confused, but then Daddy showed me. He showed me a couple of times over.

Afterwards, I cried, a lot.

10

People *are trash, Ruby,* Daddy whispers, and I wake up.

Or at least, I try to. It feels harder than it should. I feel like I am swimming, only that isn't quite right. Not swimming, not flying either. I am...I am...I don't know what I am. I can't remember words very well. My eyelids are gummed together, and my body is heavy, so, so heavy.

Consciousness creeps into me like a slow dawn, and with it, awareness of my situation.

I am strapped into a chair.

I try to open my eyelids, and feel a faint pressure against my skin. Something gelatinous, slimy, heavy, like a membrane wrapped around me, a shroud, maybe? An image of an Egyptian mummy flashes to mind, absurdly: a bandaged body.

Eventually, I manage to rip through the goo coating my lids and open my eyes. They flutter like a dying insect, then hold, but I still cannot see properly. There is a thick film of something misty covering my corneas. I blink it away, blink, blink, blink, and slowly adjust to blurry, yet harsh lighting and unfamiliar surroundings.

And then, I realise something, something alarming.

There is no air.

I cannot breathe.

It sinks in. I make myself see, make myself widen my crusted eyes further so I can really process my predicament, and it becomes clear: I cannot breathe because I am, in fact, covered from head to toe in an opaque layer of something that looks and feels like glue. Underneath it, I am naked.

There is more. My gaze travels slowly around as I become fully awake.

I am sealed inside a huge, airless glass chamber.

It is about seven feet tall by six feet wide, and shaped into a tubular form, closed off at both ends. The more I look, the more I see. The chamber is made of thick, curved glass that warps and distorts everything outside, except for one thing.

The recognisable shape of a person standing on the other side of the glass, watching me.

I panic, which is stupid, but instinct takes over and I start to hyperventilate, only to realise I am also gagged with a thick cloth that tastes of chemicals and squeaks against my teeth. My panic grows as I try, and fail, to suck air into my lungs through my nostrils instead of my mouth. But there is no air to be found. The snot-like substance coating my skin shoots up my nose as I try to inhale, and hits the back of my throat. It tastes bland, like...vaseline?

My ears pop. My head pounds. It gets worse the longer I sit there, as if something is squeezing me, as if I am underwater.

The figure in front of the chamber watches me. I can see a ghostly pale smudge through the thick glass: the person's face. I think, but I can't be sure, that it is a woman. Not that it matters. Unless I can find some air, I am going to be dead in a matter of minutes.

But wait...no, that's not right.

Am I? Really?

I am the Phoenix from the ashes.

I *can't* die, can I?

I tried it once, already, and it didn't stick.

Having said that, I haven't yet tried to suffocate myself. I've been shot and stabbed, I've been punched and thrown around, I've been hit by a train, and burned up in a car crash. But I haven't, as yet, been suffocated.

It's a new experience for me, and I hate it.

'Hello, Ruby,' a voice says, snapping me out of my panic. It is being piped into the chamber somehow via a tiny speaker on the floor. My eyes seek it out, find it, looking for a flaw in my prison. The speaker has minute holes in it, and is surrounded by a thick rubber sealant, to minimise the risk of any air coming in from around the edges of it. It dawns on me that this is a completely airtight space. Engineered that way, deliberately, by someone who clearly had me in mind when they built it.

Who has been watching me? Police? Government?

Someone else?

I scan every inch of my prison that I can see with cloudy eyes. No vents, no joins or seams, nothing but thick, heavy glass, and the tiny speaker on the floor.

The voice continues. It is female.

'My name is Wagner, but you don't need to know that. I see the tranquilizers have worn off. To be perfectly honest, I am amazed they had any effect on you at all. We gave you enough to kill ten normal women of your height and body mass, but then...well. You aren't 'normal', are you, Ruby?'

I can't answer. All I can focus on is the crunching, squeezing sensation creeping over my chest. A thin trickle of blood worms its way out of one of my ears, and down my neck to my collar bone. I understand what is happening. I am in an airtight chamber.

And I am using up all the remaining oxygen in it.

My new friend confirms my suspicions. She speaks patiently, as if addressing a room full of unruly children.

'I did a lot of camping when I was a kid, Ruby, and I learned a few things about fire. I'll lay some basic science on you, while we're getting to know each other.'

I stare through the glass. I can feel my eyes bulging. Hate glitters down there in the depths of me, but the woman behind the glass can't see it. She doesn't care, anyway.

People are trash, Daddy whispers.

I know suddenly what this is.

This is an interrogation.

Someone has finally caught up with me. I'm not really surprised. Ruby Miller is a danger to society, a threat to be neutralised. Ruby Miller killed people, a *lot* of people. She is a murderer, and a destroyer of things, and needs containing.

I fucking *hate* being contained.

'You need three things to make a fire, Ruby,' Wagner's voice continues, and I wish she would stop using my fucking name like that, like she owns it. It sounds dirty in her mouth, and I want to plug her fucking hole up with something hot and cleansing, reclaim my name, but I can't, and she knows it.

'Three things.' I can hear her mentally ticking them off, one by one.

'Heat. Well, you've got that in abundance, I think it's fair to say.'

The pressure behind my eyes continues to build. My head is pounding with pain. I jerk against my constraints. A tiny flicker of blue flame runs around my body and then snuffs out, leaving tiny curls of black smoke hanging in the chamber.

What?

I try again. *Bring the fire, Ruby,* I tell myself, and it comes, it breaks the surface of my skin, but then...it dies down, extinguishes itself, leaving behind a mounting sense of horror and grief.

My fire is gone, I think, beginning to shake violently from head to toe.

They have taken my fire from me.

I scream around my gag.

I can hear a smile develop in Wagner's voice.

'Fuel,' she continues, her strange, distorted image moving around before me, like she is pacing back and forth along the perimeter of the chamber. 'Shall we talk about fuel, Ruby?'

My nose starts to bleed, just a tiny drip, drip, drip, like a leaking tap. Wagner continues. I can tell from the tone of her voice that she is enjoying herself.

'Fuel usually means kindling, and logs, coal maybe. Except when it comes to you. When it comes to *you*, fuel means people, doesn't it? Women, children, innocent men going about their daily business. Old folk, and young. Dogs, cows, livestock. Did I say children? Yeah, children too. Do you know how many babies you've murdered, Ruby? Do you know what baby bones look like?'

Trash, whispers Daddy, and he is as furious as I am.

Wagner continues. 'Shall we talk about the town of Glenn's Ferry, Ruby? Shall we talk about how you wiped it off the face of this earth? Shall we talk about the baby bones they found, the adult bones, the teeth? Teeth don't seem to burn like the rest of a body, for some reason, I'm sure you've realised that, by now. We have a lot of teeth in storage, Ruby. It has taken our forensic anthropologists *weeks* to identify only a handful of your victims through what partial dental remains we could recover. *Weeks.* And still, there are families with nothing to bury, nothing to mourn.'

I continue to shake. Sweat beads on my forehead. The blue flame glimmers once again, snaking around my wrists and along my limbs before fizzling out impotently. I scream into my gag once more, long, and hard, emptying myself into the noise, then I choke, because my throat is clogged up with that awful sticky substance, and I collapse forward against my bonds, retching, gagging. Wagner chuckles to herself. She sounds like a woman with a plan. And so far, her plan is working.

Why don't I have a plan, I think, trying to stop myself from coughing up both my lungs, and my dripping nose-bleed intensifies.

Wagner continues.

'Back to our science lesson. Do you know what the last component of fire is, Ruby? I don't mean to be patronising, because I think you're a bright kid, really I do. But,' and here, Wagner's shadow suddenly shrinks, as if she has sat down.

'I have a confession to make.' Her voice turns friendly, conspiratorial. And I know that tone. I know it because I speak that way, myself, just before the fire comes.

Who is this woman? And where the fuck *am* I? Why does it feel like I am underground, somehow, even though I'm trapped in this glass coffin, how can I sense that? It's an impression of weight above me, of density, of heaviness, somehow. Underground. A bunker? A cave? A facility of some sort? It feels...organised.

A moot fucking point while I'm trapped in this tube, really.

'I'm afraid I'm kind of enjoying myself,' Wagner whispers, then gasps in mock surprise at her own daring. 'Is that wrong of me? I mean it's hard to feel compassion for a mass murderer, honestly, so maybe I'm overthinking things. I digress.' She sighs, her voice growing neutral once again.

'Anyway. The last component of fire, Ruby, is oxygen. Which is where *this* comes in.' She stands up, and taps the glass of the chamber that I am trapped in. The sound comes through muffled, but it still stokes my insides, stokes them good and hot.

If only I could burn on the *outside*, too.

For the first time in a long time, I feel like crying.

Bitch took my fire.

'Without oxygen, you can't burn,' Wagner finishes, and air, or no air, my rage begins to fill me from the feet up, and I have never hated anyone more in my life.

Not even my Daddy.

No oxygen.

My nosebleed grows worse, becomes a flood of salty, hot liquid that runs down into my gag, where it soaks in, and I can feel it against my lips, taste myself. I taste...weird.

Maybe I am dying after all, I think, then I smack that thought upside the head. *Stop that. You're not dying. You can't die. You've tried already. Stop being a little bitch.*

You've been in terrible situations before, and survived.

You'll survive this.

Fire, or no fire.

It's not even like I care that much if I *do* die, I'm beyond that, I'm aware that all good things come to an end eventually, and I guess I had a good second run. The first run: not so good. But I don't fear death, not anymore. I've gotten pretty comfortable with it.

It's just that...well.

I haven't really gotten started on taking the rest of the world down with me.

And I still have work to do.

I still have trash to take out.

Remembering this gives me strength. The urge to cry dissolves. The urge to kill rises up, like a two-headed cobra, rearing to strike.

That's it, Ruby.

That's it.

And to think, you were on the verge of giving up!

Stupid girl.

Hate, I realise, can be a useful survival mechanism.

Perhaps that's why my blood tastes bad. It tastes of loathing.

Wagner continues to pace, moving around and around the chamber like a lioness prowling through long grass, and if she had a tail, I imagine she would be swishing it, by now. Her body and face are still a blur to me, but I can see just enough to know that she is compact, and short, that she is probably wearing heels, based on the faint *click-clack* coming through the speaker, and dark clothing.

Then, she stands directly behind me, and I can tell from the faint prickle that sweeps up my arms that she is looking at the back of my stubbled head through the layers of thick, treated glass. She is looking at my tattoo: a phoenix, in flight, wings outspread, beak wide open. I get a sense of being judged, I get the impression that Wagner is sneering at me. Wagner is not afraid of me, and who can blame her? I'm about as threatening as a fly trapped in a spider's web right now.

Or so she thinks.

I try once more to summon fire, show her what I'm capable of, but it spurts, and ripples, then fizzles out.

'Every time you do that,' Wagner says, and I can tell from her tone that her lip is curled, 'You waste more oxygen. Don't you get that? Or are you as dumb-fuck stupid as you are evil?'

Evil. The word sinks into my brain.

Am I evil?

I think back to Glenns Ferry, to an entire town wiped off the map.

Yeah, I guess I must be. In the traditional sense of the word.

Evil.

Huh.

Evil or not, my existence is an insult to Wagner, I know it. I know women like her. I don't know why she is doing this to me, or who the fuck she works for, but I know women like her. Power-hungry control freaks with personality issues. And I would bet my ass that she is jealous of me, too. That she considers me undeserving of my power. Wager can hate too, it seems. Yeah, of course she does. Of course Wagner hates me, because she wants what I have. She wants power over life and death, but she is weak and human, and that makes her fallible. And she wants to hurt me for this.

'This chamber,' Wagner continues, 'has been custom designed, just for you. Isn't that nice of us?' She continues her circle, coming back to stand in front of me. How I wish I could get a clear view of her, make proper eye contact.

'It's an oxygen deprivation tank, in case you hadn't figured that out, and we've sucked almost all the juice out of it, because without oxygen, as we have already established, fire doesn't burn. Without oxygen, technically, you shouldn't be able to breathe. You *should* be experiencing symptoms of severe hypoxia, right now, but because you are what we in the industry like to call a Grade A Freak, you seem to be kind of okay in your little goldfish bowl. A bit puffy and red, if I'm honest, but I was kind of hoping for something more...dramatic. I was kind of hoping you would suffocate to death, but never mind. If we can't kill you, it's enough to see that you can't burn. For now.'

I feel thankful that she is not able to see the amount of pain and discomfort I am in. Despite the rage that pounds through my veins, I feel like deep-fried shit on toast, and I've already died once before, so that's saying something.

Wager presses her face suddenly against the thick glass, smooshing her cheek hard into the chamber wall so I can just about make out one of her eyes, glaring at me.

'How does it feel, Ruby?' She asks. 'How does it feel to be out of control?'

And I think: *I was never in control in the first place, bitch.*

Another huge, rippling convulsion wracks my body. I might not be suffocating as quickly as Wagner wants, but as the air is slowly sucked from the chamber, and my body reacts, *something* is happening to me. I'm not sure what it is, I'm not sure it's death, not yet, but it's...something. And it doesn't feel good. It feels...

'Oh, by the way, Ruby. I was wondering.'

Wondering what, you malicious cunt? I'm going to eat that fucking tongue of yours when I get out of here, just you wait and see.

'How would you feel if I asked you a few questions about your Father?'

My entire body runs cold. Everything in me stops to make room for what Wagner just said.

What?

What does she know about Daddy?

She senses my stillness, and throws back her head, a small bark of laughter escaping her mouth. 'Oh, god, you killer kids are all the fucking same. Daddy issues. No, scratch that. *Responsibility* issues. Because it's always someone else's fault, isn't it? Mommy beat me. Daddy couldn't keep it in his pants. Uncle Dan sold me drugs. The mailman flashed his dick at me, etcetera etcetera. You think that gives you a free pass to act out any way you want, Ruby? I mean, sure, what your father did to you was not right, not at all, not by anyone's standards, but do you know how many kids out there in the world start out life the exact same way you did, Ruby? Or how many kids there are who had it worse? Kids who *don't* go on to become murdering, spree-killer psychopaths? Do you? Do you think it gives you some fucking right to behave the way you do? Because I don't.'

She moves closer to the chamber, placing something up against the glass that she knows I can't see. If I had to guess, based on the vague shape and size of it, I would say it was a photograph, and I'm beginning to understand what she is headed for, conversationally.

Obviously, someone has been to my old house, and obviously, someone has been in the cellar, and obviously, someone has finally found Daddy.

Except that can't be right, Daddy isn't dead, Daddy lives in my head, at least, that's what I've always assumed. Daddy is the voice that stops me from sleeping at night, Daddy is the gasoline on the fire. Daddy is…

Daddy is…

Yeah, okay, okay.

Daddy is dead.

'I must say, you did quite a number on him Ruby,' Wagner purrs, enjoying herself. 'Quite a number, although I have to ask: how come you didn't barbeque him like all the others?'

I cannot reply. I cannot tell her that Daddy was *before* the car crash. Before the change.

Before the gift of fire.

If I'd had my power before, my life would have been very different.

This hurts to think about.

Wagner's shadow moves, shifts its weight, and the photograph remains slapped against the glass, virtually indistinguishable as anything except a dark, oblong-shaped blob.

'You cannot see what I'm holding in my hand, but I can,' my tormentor continues. 'It's a crime scene photo, taken in the basement of the house you ran away from, your childhood home. It's a shame you can't see it, actually, because I wonder if looking at the mess you made of the man who gave you life might not sober you up a little. Make you question some of your life choices a bit. Are you capable of remorse, Ruby? Are you? I don't think so.'

And in the back of my mind, Daddy whispers: *What did you do to me, Ruby?*

What did you do?

Well, that's easy, Daddy, I think back. *I got tired of you sticking parts of your body into parts of me where they didn't belong, so I pushed you down the basement stairs one afternoon in a fit of blind rage, and when you got to the bottom, cracking your head open on the concrete floor, I followed you, rolled you over with one foot, and beat the living shit out of you with a tyre iron.*

Then, when your face was no more than splinter and jelly, I buried you under a pile of cardboard and junk, packed a bag, jumped into my Pontiac, and got the hell out of Dodge.

Remembering all this for the first time feels...strange. Like it all happened to someone else, not me. Like I am no longer in the glass chamber, but outside my old house, looking in through the window at a different type of Ruby, a Ruby with long hair and bruises on her thighs and nothing in her heart except fear and desperation.

I'd kind of forgotten about her, what with the car accident and everything that followed.

Would that Ruby be afraid of this Ruby? It is an odd question to ask myself.

Wagner should be afraid of me, but she isn't. She should be cowering in my shadow, but instead, she is taking pleasure in my weakness. I hate this. I hate it with the fire of a thousand burning suns. I jerk violently, straining against my bonds, but it is futile. Without my flames, I am just another girl, just another normal person, with blood soaking into her clothes and a sick, sour feeling in her belly, because what Wagner is saying is right, I am out of control, and, and…

Daddy's dead body flashes into my mind. His face, caved inwards. His brains, wet and loose upon the hard, cold floor.

His hands, resting lightly up by his head.

His perfectly manicured fingernails, covered in blood and winking at me in the light of the basement.

Another scream rips out of me, more of a roar this time, Ruby is roaring, her eyelids are puffy and tight, her lips cracked and bleeding, and if Wagner could see through the glass properly, she would see a thin, weak, blue light rippling along the backs of my hands. My fire is trying. It is trying despite everything. I wonder what Wagner is feeling right now as she watches me. She has a tiger by the tail, and I bet it feels good to her, I bet it gets her all warm and wet between the legs.

'Did I touch on a nerve, Ruby?' Wagner lowers her voice to a soft hiss.

I stop shaking and twitching. I grow very, very still.

'Can you feel it, freak? Can you feel the effects of the chamber on your body? Maybe I'll just keep sucking all the air out until your lungs rupture and fail. Even abominations of nature like you have to breathe air, don't they? I don't particularly need to keep you alive. No-one is going to be mad at me for putting an end to you, Ruby Miller.'

But I can't die, stupid, I think, even as black spots swim across my vision. My memories dance, lazily. There is a painting I'd seen once, in an art book. An old one, famous. A white bird...a parrot, trapped inside a glass dome. There is a pump attached to the dome, a pump that is sucking the air out while an audience of men in wigs and women in satin dresses and small, distressed children looked on. An experiment. The men want to see how long it takes for the bird to die without air. The painting is shadowy, rich, the bird's death throes picked out in high relief. A study of light and dark.

Basic science.

I am the bird in the glass dome.

Except…

Except…

Think, Ruby! Daddy shouts, and it comes to me then, a bolt of clarity.

Basic science also says the dead don't come back to life.

I am above basic science, I realise.

I smile, suddenly. I smile through a mouthful of my own tainted blood. My mouth works behind the sodden gag, opening, closing, a fish out of water. A ringing noise grows in my ears.

I feel heat building in my chest.

No.

No, the bird will not *die.*

For a little while, I had forgotten who I was.

For a little while, I had believed Wagner's lies. She had me thinking that I was just like everyone else, that I need the same air she breathes.

But I don't.

I am still alive in this chamber because I don't.

I am Ruby Miller.

I have come back from the dead.

I can summon fire at will.

The rules do not apply to me.

Basic science can go fuck itself.

I chuckle, the heat rising and building, the flames that always hide inside of me licking at the back of my throat, burning away the horrible goo sliding down my gullet. I could weep with joy as my skin ignites properly for the first time since waking, as my headache fades, as my lungs fill with fire. I could weep, but I will not, because I have shit to do, and crying is a waste of my time.

Instead, I erupt.

Wagner is buried under a foot of concrete, glass and insulation when I find her. I am naked, and glowing. My lungs are full and hot, and I feel the hum of insatiable energy under my skin.

How could I have forgotten this? I wonder, but that will have to be something I come back to later.

First, Wagner.

Dust hangs thick in the air, and sporadic showers of debris rattle down all around me like hail. In the distance, an alarm is ringing, loud and insistent. I can see corridors leading out of the collapsed room, three in total. It's hard to see much else through the dust, but I get an impression of size, of a deliberate, grid-pattern layout. Definitely a facility of some sort, or a lair. And, judging by the thick seams of rock I can see in the corridor walls, definitely underground.

I dig through rubble with my bare hands until Wagner's head is exposed, then stop.

The woman blinks painfully.

'Oh, there you are,' I say, pulsing with light. 'I couldn't see you properly before, not through all that glass.'

Wagner shrinks back as far as she is able, but she is pinned to the floor by a broken concrete ceiling beam. She won't live long, I can tell. Her face is white with dust and ash and embedded with thick studs of glass from where the glass chamber exploded outwards. A shard of metal has lodged itself in her right ear. Blood bubbles on her lips, and she rattles as she breathes, struggling for air. I chuckle at the irony. Wagner's lungs have collapsed under the weight of the beam.

Now the shoe is on the other fucking foot.

I lower my face so that it is right next to Wagner's.

'Turns out I don't need oxygen, you piece of shit,' I whisper, running a hand through the other woman's short, sticky hair. She has a short, almost military style cut, like a crew cut only longer at the sides, and her face is exactly as I imagined it: broad features, a strong jawline, piercing grey eyes.

Wagner rattles out another laboured breath, watching me warily and flinching under my caress.

'How about you tell me what this fucking place is, before you die, hmm?' I ask, plucking a hair from her head. 'How about you tell me who you work for?' I yank another hair out, and let it fall to the ground. I'm not sure why I am doing this, but I am enjoying the discomfort it brings to my enemy. I want her last moments on this earth to be as uncomfortable as humanly possible.

'You're…' Wagner chokes, and blood sprays out in a fine mist across my face.

'Yes?'

'You're...a...fucking...freak...' Wagner manages, and her eyes roll back in her head.

Sticks and stones, I think, and clamp my fingers around the roots of Wagner's hair. I smile a vulpine, lethal smile.

'Eat me,' I say, jamming my tongue hard down the other woman's throat. Fire roars into Wagner, and I grip harder, savouring the smell as my captor cooks, roasting from the inside out.

I move through a network of tunnels and corridors carved directly into what seems to be a huge natural fissure, deep in the heart of what I can only assume is a mountain somewhere in America, but this is only based on the fact that the scant signage I can see hung around the place is written in english. Otherwise, I could be anywhere on the known fucking planet.

Not that it matters. Soon, I'll be out in the sun again.

And then I have some work to do.

Occasionally, I meet someone running in the opposite direction. Usually, they are armed, although nobody seems to have the wherewithal to use a tranq gun on me this time. Even if they did, I have learned my lesson. I wear a coat of fire around my naked body as I walk, for I will never be caught unawares again. Let them shoot whatever shit they want in my direction. It won't get past the flames.

I won't let anything past the flames ever again.

I burn as I go, manipulating the fire with hungry hands, sending it down this corridor and that passageway, opening doors, cooking people alive before they even have a second to process what's happening to them. As the word gets out in the warren that Ruby is on the loose, doors burst open all over, men and women scattering like rabbits before me, but I am done with being nice, I am done with letting bygones be bygones and sleeping dogs lie and whatever other bullshit slogans people have come up with over the years to excuse weakness, everyone here is trash, everyone here is in my way, and that's their fucking fault, not mine.

No survivors, Ruby, Daddy whispers in my red-hot mind.

It's a missive I can finally get on board with.

Or at least, that's what I tell myself.

Until I hear the girl screaming.

She's in a small room off a narrow side-passage, a passage full of metal-plated doors that look like prison cell doors, rather than the meeting rooms and test-labs I've encountered so far. This looks like a jail corridor, and this triggers a new wave of fury in me, because they tried to cage me, these motherfuckers, they tried to silence me, they tried to take my fire, and now they're doing it to someone else.

For that reason alone I pause, coming to a rest outside the first cell door. The screams ring out from behind it. They sound familiar, or the voice making them does at any rate.

'She's not my friend!' The girl screams, over and over again. 'I've never seen her before in my life until yesterday! I keep telling you this! She came into the diner and...and...'

Cat. Was that her name? Pretty, blonde. She hit on me in the diner, bought me a root beer before all hell broke loose.

In a different time, I might have bought her one back.

One touch of my hand, and the cell door melts, slumps

to the ground in a molten, glowing pile, revealing the room within. Inside, one woman and two men are rigorously torturing the blonde, who is tied to a chair much like I was only an hour ago. She is also naked, and her captors are taking it in turns to press an electric cattle prod to the soft skin of her thighs, ducking and diving as the girl screams and strains against her bonds. From the looks of it, they've already administered it elsewhere on her body too. She shudders in pain, her entire body drawing tight as a string every time the electrified prongs come into contact with her skin, and I wonder again:

Who the fuck are these people?

They stop when I make my entrance, whirling about in surprise, faces draining of colour.

'The fuck is this?' I ask, more out of curiosity than anything else, and I am so bright none of them can look at me.

'Help me,' the girl whispers. 'It doesn't matter how many times I say it, they just don't believe me. For the love of god, *help me!*'

No survivors, Daddy says again, more mournfully this time.

Cat's eyes roll wildly in her head, and her chest heaves. 'Help me,' she whispers, again. I remember, suddenly, being naked in the desert. I remember asking a woman with purple hair for help, because I was alone, and afraid, and vulnerable. She spat in my face, and her friends tried to take me, against my will.

I think about this as I stare at the girl's terrified face.

No survivors.

But I think I'll make an exception.

Just this once.

13

The blonde follows me as I burn my way through the warren. She keeps a healthy distance behind. Every now and then, I hear her crying, but trying to keep it quiet. She must be in pain. I look back over my shoulder. She has a wound on her inner thigh that I didn't notice before. It leaks down her legs, leaving a slick wet trail behind her. If she isn't careful, she will bleed out. If I was that kind of person, I might stop for a moment, help her walk, let her lean on me, maybe even cauterise the wound, but I am not that kind of person, and she should count herself lucky I'm letting her live, for I am not the merciful type. She senses this, I know, she senses that I could change my mind at any given moment, so she keeps back, out of reach. Smart.

Soon, we are the only living things left in the place, whatever this place is, whoever it was built by. And we find ourselves, eventually, at the bottom of a sloping access ramp. At the end of the ramp, I can see a large, square door, like a garage door, only more industrial in scale and build. A tiny strip of bright light outlines this door, and I breathe a sigh of relief, because even I am getting tired.

I want out.

The door disintegrates, and is replaced with a brilliant, cobalt blue sky. I can see we are high, really high, and upon emerging, naked as the day I was born, into the daylight, I can see my guess was right: the warren is borrowed into the side of a mountain, perhaps taking advantage of a cave that had once existed there naturally. Which mountain, I couldn't tell you, but I don't care. I don't need a name.

I am free.

The sun finally touches my face. It feels good. It feels *real* fucking good. I realise I don't much like being in the dark, I don't much like being underground.

I have to be out, out where wings can soar.

I scan the surroundings, looking for trouble. All is quiet. A gentle wind blows around us, and Cat starts to shiver in earnest. The mountain has to be a few thousand metres high, judging from the treeline that starts a good way below us, and the faint dusting of snow on the peak. I wonder how the fuck all those people working in the warren get up here, until I see a helipad sprayed onto a flat area of rock off to my left.

I wonder how long it will be before someone spots the smoke pouring out of the mouth of the warren, roiling up into the sky in a black, noxious column.

Not long, I'll wager.

No rest for the wicked, Ruby, I think to myself, and turn, looking for the easiest path down the mountain side.

Cat, exhausted, slides to the floor and sits, holding her hands against her bare, bleeding thigh. Her hands aren't enough, however, and her blood continues to pump out of her, forming a thin, trickling stream, a stream that winds downhill, which is where I want to go.

She tries to keep her conversation light. Again, this is smart. She knows that if she asks me for any more help, I might lose my cool. She senses that I've had enough of what other people want. Cat is a clever woman. Her survival instincts are keen. I can respect that, if I try hard enough.

'Who the fuck *were* those people? They seemed...organised.' She pants, clenching her jaw in an effort to stay conscious. Her skin has gone an unhealthy shade of pale.

I stare off into the distance for a moment, mind elsewhere. I still don't have a plan, and this bothers me. Where to go now? How long before more people come after me? Does it matter? I can't be touched, I've proved that to myself. Why wait to start on the work that needs doing?

No reason, only…

I'm tired.

I could use a little rest.

A glob of something works its way up my throat: some of the slime they coated me in. I hazard a guess that they thought it was flame-retardant, whatever it was. I hawk it up and spit it out, and stare in surprise at what lies on the ground by my big toe, coated in goo.

A tooth.

More to the point: one of *my* teeth.

I frown, working my tongue into the empty spot the tooth has left behind. I hadn't noticed it was loose before.

'I don't think they were government, but they sure behaved like it,' I reply, thoughtfully. Then, I realised what I'm doing. I'm letting my guard down, taking my eye off the ball. I'm holding a fucking conversation with another human being, instead of doing what I should be doing, and wiping their stain clean off the soil with my fire.

I straighten up, clench my fists.

Cat sees the flames in my eyes, and tries to distract me

from any murderous thoughts I might be harbouring. I wonder what that's like, to feel one's life hanging in the balance.

Invincibility has its downsides, although I don't consider a lack of empathy something I need to worry about, right now.

'They had...things down there in that place. In those cells, next to me. I saw, when they were carrying me along the corridor. I saw...shit that shouldn't exist. Like a boy, with a rat's ears, and a rat's tail. Fucking teeth like a...well, yeah. A rat. I saw him.'

I would have laughed at her once, but that was before I became a freak.

I am not sure how I feel about the idea of other freaks coming to town.

Nevertheless, her plan is working. My desire to obliterate her wanes a little.

'It doesn't matter,' I say, half to myself, and half to her. 'They are all dead, now. And I need to go. I have things to do.' I begin walking down the mountainside. My bare feet track through a thin stream of Cat's blood, and it feels warm. My footprints turn red behind me.

'Wait!' the desperate woman cries out, terrified. She has realised something.

'If you leave me here, I'll die!'

It is true. We are in the middle of nowhere. She is bleeding heavily, on the brink of unconsciousness, and can't walk, can't stand, can't support her own bodyweight. She won't be able to find water by herself, or shelter, or food. I have no idea where we are, or how close we are to a road, or a town, or any type of civilisation. I suspect that even if the girl could drag herself down the mountain and find a house or a road and flag down a car, she isn't about to trust anyone who lives in a forty mile radius of this place. I agree with her on that front. Neither of us want to end up back underground.

That doesn't leave the kid much choice, but I am past giving a shit. Soon, this entire country will be ash and smoke, anyhow. She's better off giving up, letting herself die on the side of this hill. At least the sky will be blue as she goes.

'Ruby!' The girl shouts, her voice harsh and desperate. *'Please!'*

Who are you kidding, lady, I think. *I am a mass murderer. I'm beyond emotion. I can't feel shit, anymore. I'm not going to save you.*

'Why let me live, only to leave me?' She pleads, and her strength is fading, her words thick and heavy in her mouth.

Who knows? Who cares? I don't owe her any explanation.

I.

Don't.

Owe.

Her.

Shit.

Only, I find myself slowing.

'Please.'

I find myself turning, looking back at her, at her ghostly face and fragile, naked body.

I remember a girl, bloodied and terrified, naked, in a desert.

'Please.'

I remember another girl, a younger girl, cowering in the corner of her bedroom, looking up at her fate as he loomed large and red-faced above her.

I go back.

14

Her wound is easy enough to cauterize. The trick is controlling the fire and restraining myself, because it would be so damn easy to take her entire leg off, if I had a mind to, so easy to reduce her to a small mound of ash and blow her off the palm of my hand, if I wanted.

But that would defeat the purpose of this uncharacteristic moment of charity.

Whatever the fuck that is.

She doesn't ask me why I am helping her, again, because she is a smart kid. Kid- she's probably more than a few years older than me, but her size and those big eyes make her appear younger. No, she doesn't ask me why I'm doing what I'm doing, and I don't ask her what made the four inch hole in her skin. I can figure it out for myself, pretty much- it was something serrated, and it made a hell of a mess as it worked through her flesh. I'd feel angry about it on her behalf if I hadn't already obliterated the fuckers who did it to her.

And, if I had the capacity to feel things on the behalf of others.

But I don't.

Ruby is all about Ruby, these days.

Or is she?

She shudders as I seal the gash in her thigh, averting her gaze. Her injury doesn't seem to bother her as much as being naked in front of me does, something I find amusing, because a body is just a body, in my mind. It doesn't much matter what it looks like, only whether or not it can get you where you need to go.

Except I didn't always used to think like that.

Especially when Daddy was driving *my* body.

Anyway, I'm glad she doesn't ask, because I don't know what the fuck there is to say in answer to that question. Why help her? I don't know why, really I don't. Maybe I figure, what's the point in saving her in the first place, like she said, only to let her die? Maybe I am feeling contrary. Maybe I want to see if I really *am* evil, all the way through, or maybe I'm wondering if my evil comes in spots, like rotten patches on a dropped apple. You can cut the bad bits away, and still have a half-way decent apple left behind.

But thinking like that is dangerous. Thinking like that is weakness.

I have no time left for weakness.

We walk, once she has recovered a little. I let her lean on me. She limps, and shivers with cold. It's a cold I do not feel.

Eventually, we reach a thin tree-line, made up of twiggy, thirsty looking saplings and scrubby brush plants. Cat spots an opportunity, stops, pulls away from me and wrestles a sapling out of the ground. She is stronger than she looks, despite everything going the wrong way for her.

Resilient, I think the word is. She strips the sapling of its leaves with trembling fingers and uses it as a crutch as we continue on our path down. She doesn't want to lean on me, not anymore.

Smart girl, I think again.

But it's not like I have a crush on her, or anything.

THE TREES GROW THICKER, fleshier, the saplings and scrub giving way to deep green firs and pines. Grass replaces the scree underfoot, and birds start to sing.

The sky stays blue between the pine needles.

And I still can't figure out why I haven't burned the whole fucking mountain, down, yet.

Maybe it's the girl, Cat. Maybe she calms me.

Or maybe I'm just gathering my strength.

Lotta maybes coming out of me today, I muse.

After a mile of hiking through woodland, we come across a cabin. Empty, but well cared for, a holiday home, or writer's retreat, maybe. Windows shuttered, a small outhouse a few yards from the main building. Cute, functional.

Cat speaks.

'I need clothes,' she says. I knew it was coming.

'You don't have to stay with me,' she continues, and her face looks haunted. She wants rid of me. 'I should be able to manage, from here. For a while, at least.'

I smile, bitterly. And here was me thinking we were sharing a special moment.

She doesn't wait for my reply, simply limps off toward the cabin. I watch her go. I see her head held high, despite her fear. I see resolve and determination.

I see her stumble, see her makeshift crutch catch on something on the ground, see her injured leg give way.

I see her fall, flat on her face.

She does not get up.

I sigh.

THE CABIN IS COSY, or at least it is once I light a fire in the stone hearth built into the middle of the place. The smell of pine fills my nostrils. It reminds me of being a kid, of holidaying in the mountains with Mom and Daddy before…

Before Daddy began to play his special games with me.

I realise it's been a while since I last heard Daddy's voice in my head, which is a relief. I hate that he lives rent-free in my mind the way he does, I hate that I never know when he is going to start whispering sweet nothings into the spaces between my ears again, but I'll enjoy the peace while I have it.

I leave the girl, Cat, asleep by the fire. She is exhausted, and running a fever. I left it too long to cauterise her wound, and the infection looks like it has taken a firm hold. I figure all she needs is rest, that her body will try and sort everything else out while she sleeps.

There is a small closet near the bed pushed up against one wall, and I rifle through it, looking for clothes, because even I'm starting to get bored of the sight of my own tits swinging around without restraint. I don't have high hopes for finding much, but fate is funny that way, and at the bottom of the closet I uncover a huge, faded plaid shirt and a pair of mom jeans which are too big for me around the waist and too short in the leg, but I can make them work. Under that, I find an old t-shirt and a pair of board shorts that look like they belonged once to a kid. Cat can have those when she wakes up.

As I get dressed, I notice something on my ankle, something I haven't seen before. It is a sore, about the size and diameter of a coin. It confuses me. Usually, wounds heal on my body within moments of them having been made. I poke my finger into the raw spot. It doesn't hurt, but it shouldn't be fucking there, either. I think back to my tooth, lying in a puddle of phlegm and slime.

What is happening to me now?

And, more importantly:

Why the fuck am I wasting time here?

But I've gotten good at silencing the voices in my head, these days, so I tell myself to pipe the fuck down, and make my way to the kitchenette on the other side of the cabin.

Because I'm thirsty.

For so much.

NIGHT FALLS as Cat wakes up, which is a little act of unconscious rebellion on her part that appeals to me, somehow. Waking up when everything else is bedding down for the night. I know she hasn't planned it that way, but I'm looking for things to hang onto, because I don't like to admit that I've been sitting on a chair by the fire for the last three hours watching her sleep. I don't like to admit it, because even I know it's kind of fucking creepy, but she is growing on me, this petite little thing. She's growing on me so much I even covered her with a blanket while she slept, to protect her dignity.

At least I think that's why I did it. It's kind of hard to tell why I do anything much, these days. My brain has been rewired by hate for so long, I'm having a hard time identifying anything else, feelings wise. It might be why she fascinates me so much, this girl. Because she's making me feel things that aren't death, and fire, and revenge, and anger. It's not that I don't enjoy those feelings, because I do. It's not that I don't intend to act out my feelings, the way I've planned to, because I am set on a path now, and that path leads to only one place. I know this. I'm reconciled with it.

But.

But.

There is something compelling about being a different type of Ruby. Even if only for a little while.

I chew over all this as Cat sits up, groggy, and registers my presence.

'You're still here,' she says. She does not look happy about it.

'You're welcome,' I say in response, and she flinches. I roll my eyes. 'Jesus, relax. I'm not going to hurt you. I would have done it by now, if I was. I would have let you bleed out on the mountain.'

She stares at me, and maybe its the extra confidence that the blanket gives her, because she sticks her chin out, anger dancing freely across her pretty face.

'And what, we're best friends now? Because you didn't let me die? Big fucking whoop.' She snorts. And I am momentarily bowled over by her sass. She knows what I am capable of, but she is past caring, now. I helped her, and she thinks this makes her immune to me, safer, somehow. She's also got a recklessness about her that she didn't have before. Like she's seen some shit, and come out the other side, changed.

I kind of like that.

I know how it feels.

Daddy chooses that moment to mumble something in

the back of my mind, but I push him away. *Not now, Daddy. Not now.*

His voice retreats, reluctantly, but he'll be back, I know he will. He always comes back. That's just his way. He is persistent.

They say we turn into our parents, eventually, whether we like it or not.

I don't like that idea. Not one little bit.

'I found some food in the cupboards- a tin of beans, a packet soup. You should probably eat,' I say, wondering what it feels like to be hungry. I lost my appetite weeks ago, in fact, I cannot remember the last time I ate anything at all. I can remember the last time I had a drink, because I am still thirsty, all the time, but my body seems to run just fine without food. Another peculiarity of this new version of me that doesn't make any biological sense, just like the fact that I don't need oxygen in my lungs the way normal people do, another peculiarity, but there we are. Life doesn't have to make sense, I know that now. I remember seeing that on a poster somewhere, once, when I was younger, and it stuck with me. The poster said *'To demand sense is the hallmark of nonsense,'* and that sentence feels a little fancy, sure, but it also feels like a way-cry, somehow. We shouldn't expect life to make sense. We just make our own truths, and there is something liberating in that.

Or at least there will be, once I've started reshaping the world.

But not for a little while. For now, I want to sit in this cabin, and talk to this angry, pissed-off girl, and enjoy being a different Ruby for a hot minute or two.

'I don't want to eat,' she says. 'I feel sick. I am sick.'

I shrug. 'Suit yourself,' I say. 'There's scotch in the cupboard over the sink. And some clothes over there, if you're still feeling shy.'

She glares at me, and shrugs off the blanket, slowly rising to her feet and crossing the cabin to where I left the t-shirt and shorts. She still looks in a bad way: the wound on her thigh is a nasty colour around the cauterized scab, and the rest of her is covered in bruises and small burn marks from the electric cattle prod the people in suits tortured her with, back in the warren. Her fever has gone down, a little, but she still shivers, and is pale, her cheeks looking hollow, dark circles creeping down her face from beneath her eyes. She dresses as quickly as she can, slipping on the shorts with visible relief, wincing as the fabric drags up past her wound. The shirt fits her well, and I try not to notice how it sits tight across her breasts.

She catches me watching her, and it feels so good to see fury in another person, because I am kind of getting tired of being the only one.

'What now?' She asks, swaying unsteadily as she faces me. 'We have a nice cosy drink? Play Monopoly? Talk about ourselves?'

I smile, enjoying her discomfort.

'Why not?' I say.

She does not expect that.

15

There is no Monopoly to be found in the cabin, but there is a pack of cards. We play hearts, because that's the only game I can get the hang of quickly. Cat explains the rules to me several times before I get a decent hold of them, each time getting more and more frustrated with me, which I allow, because its like having a mirror held up to my own bad nature, and I'm surprisingly on board for it, considering everything that has led me here.

But I've been thinking about this, while I lay cards down carefully on a small table by the fire. Because, back when it was just me and my Pontiac, I'd been headed for a life like this. Quiet, peace, a readjustment of my horizons to something less onerous than 'Avoid Daddy', which is what my life had become, before I stoved his head in with a tyre iron.

Cat swigs at the bottle of scotch, and two crazy red spots of booze-flush sprout on her cheeks. She looks like a doll that's been attacked with lipstick, and the fire-light catches in her eyes, making them glassy.

I absent-mindedly rub the sore patch on my ankle with the big toe of my other foot. Is it me, or is it growing bigger?

Whatever. More importantly, I'm losing at cards.

I don't like losing, I realise.

Then, without warning, because she has drunk enough, because she has reached her limits, because she is winning at hearts and she takes that as her cue, who knows the fuck why, Cat asks a question.

'Why did you do it?' She says, staring me full in the face. 'Glenns Ferry, all those people. Why?'

The game is over. I toss my hand of cards into the fire-place, watch as they blacken and curl, then disappear up the chimney in a trail of bright sparks. A small thrill tickles my belly. It's been too long since I last destroyed something.

And even though I'm made of it, I'll never tire of looking at fire.

'Are you even listening?' Cat says, her voice heavy with emotion.

I think she is trying to provoke me, although I can't be sure. Her survival instincts have become skewed. She doesn't strike me as the suicidal type, so I can only assume she is being brave, instead. Speaking up for what's right. What she thinks she is going to achieve, I don't know. Is she going to try and shame me into feeling something? Guilt? Remorse? *That ship sailed long ago, sweetie,* I think, but I indulge her anyway.

'Because I got angry.'

'That's it? You got angry, so you murdered hundreds of innocent people?'

I prized the scotch bottle from her cold fingers. As soon as I touch the neck of the bottle, it warms up. Soon it will shatter, unable to take the constant stress of my heat. But that's okay. I can make a good enough dent in it before it does.

'That's it.'

'And you don't feel…' Her chest heaves in and out with righteousness. She hates me, but instead of letting it offend me, I find I am drawn to her even more.

'I don't feel anything. Hard for people to understand, but it's true. I guess I'm just…removed from it all.'

Her mouth works at the problem. 'You're right,' she snaps, throwing her own cards down with force upon the table top. 'I don't understand it.'

I shrug. 'Guess you're just a better person than I am, then.'

'No, that's not it,' she blazes, and I swig from the scotch bottle as she leans towards me over the top of the cards. 'That's a bullshit excuse to save you from having to deal with what you did, Ruby Miller. Denial ain't just a river in Egypt.'

'Denial? Or just truth? I don't owe anyone anything, do I? I don't owe anyone shit. Why should I care who lives or dies?'

People are trash, Daddy whispers. How like him to choose this moment to enter the fray.

Fuck you, Daddy, I think, but despite myself, I find my mood shifting to something uglier than it was a moment before.

'You *should* care, because if you don't, what even is the fucking point? You can be better than all the bad things that have happened to you, I should know.' So there is a history, then. Good. It hasn't all been roses for blondie.

'That's not been my experience.'

'Well *my* experience is not *your* experience, and I'm glad for it, because I'd hate to be… you.' She gestures at me with a curled lip. She has the bit between her teeth now, fuelled by scotch and despair and, I suspect, her own sense of bewilderment at what happened to her down in the warren. She blames me, and she is right to do so, because if I hadn't walked into that diner, she'd be tucked up in bed, safe at home.

'You think I don't get angry?' She continues, arms waving around all over the place, windmilling her frustration. And I realise I've seen this before. This is what Daddy used to do, he used to gesticulate just like this when he was telling me what a shitty thing being alive was, or how terrible other people were.

The ugliness growing in me rises.

'Because I do. Women get angry all the fucking time, Ruby, we just don't wear it on our fucking sleeves as much as we should. We've been told that to be angry is wrong, but you and I both know that's bullshit. Anger feels kind of...useful, I don't know. It's how we know something needs fixing. But my Mom always told me anger wasn't very lady-like. She still hasn't figured out that I have no interest in being lady-like.' She snorts.

I wish she'd get to the fucking point. She is starting to bore me.

'Point is, you got a second shot, didn't you? Not many of us get that opportunity. You've got this power, you've got this...invincible thing going on. You going to waste it by murdering your way through the rest of eternity? You're going to live forever Ruby, have you thought about that? About how boring violence gets, after a while? You're entitled to your anger. You're not entitled to take it out on the world at large. Do that, and you're just...I dunno, a fucking patron saint for everything toxic and bad. Tyler Durden. Thanos. The fucking Joker. With tits.'

'Fuck you,' I say, pleasantly, but she is so lost in her own certainty that she doesn't hear me.

'The kicker of it is, I don't think you're an inherently bad person.' She uses that revelation like a weapon, but I don't feel the sting the way she wants me to.

Her virtuousness does make her pretty, though.

'I don't give much of a fuck what you think.'

She continues, undeterred. I think she's verging on delirium.

'I think a lot of things happened to you, sure, that much is really fucking obvious. I think you're a product of your past. I think you've got shit you're working through. But I don't think you're evil. A psychopath, maybe. Or a sociopath. I don't know, I never studied any of that stuff well enough to know *what* to call you. But I know a bit about people. And I don't think you're evil. I don't know exactly what the fuck you are, but I've seen evil. It's different.'

I shook my head, look down at my hands. I feel...strange. Like I'm not really in the room. I realise Cat's face is pushed up, close to mine. I can smell scotch on her breath. Her eyes are huge, her pupils dilated.

'Please don't kill me,' she says then, ruining the moment. Because she means it. She really thinks I am going to incinerate her for speaking her mind.

Well, maybe she's right.

'I'm not going to kill you,' I lie, trying and failing to get a handle on the emotions mixing in my heart. 'I think...' I laugh, bitterly. 'I that's the nicest fucking thing anyone has ever said to me, if I'm being honest.'

Cat stares back at me. Sweat coats her face, and she shudders. Her mouth is dry and grey in colour. A thin red crack dissects her lower lip.

'Fuck, well if that's the case, Ruby, no wonder you are the way you are,' she croaks.

'And how am I?' We're getting down to it, now. *Is this foreplay?*

What am I thinking?

Trash, trash, trash, Daddy croons.

Cat swallows.

'People aren't born bad,' she says, eventually. 'They just aren't. They turn bad, or are made bad. I think underneath the fire, there is something good. Someone good. There has to be.'

I look away, unable to hold her gaze any longer. She is not just pretty, but beautiful in her convictions, in her strength. She is the sort of girl I should have grown up to be, and it hurts to look at her. It hurts to be near her. It hurts to think about another possible Ruby, one who wasn't moulded by Daddy's tidy hands.

The ugliness stirs again.

'You don't know shit,' I say, more to regain some control over my emotions than anything else.

'I know you saved me. I asked you to help me, and you did.'

'I did, didn't I?'

And then I can't control it anymore. It's been so long since I felt tenderness, since I touched anyone in a gentle way. I take a deep breath, and grab her sick, sweaty face with my hands, and press my mouth into hers.

She tastes…

Sour.

Hands slam into my chest, pushing me away. My mouth rips away from hers, tiny sparks like fireflies flaring in the air between our lips, then dying out.

'Get the fuck off me!' Her face is a picture of panic and anger.

There it is, Daddy says.

My heart sinks like a stone.

She rears backwards, disgust written plain on her face.

'You think because you didn't let me die you earned the right to stick your tongue in my mouth? Fuck no!'

'But you said...I saved your life. You said yourself, I'm not a bad person...'

'My fucking body, my fucking rules. I don't care how many fucking people you've killed.'

I stare at her. Her words make me feel dizzy: *my body, my rules.*

It isn't that easy.

It is never that easy.

My body, *Daddy's* rules.

And I'm jealous of her, I realise. I am jealous of Cat, because she didn't grow up the way I did, she doesn't understand that I was never allowed to make rules. Only follow them.

The ugliness has trebled in size. I can feel it filling out my skin. I look down, and a thin blue layer of flame has sprouted from my pores. I embrace it, remembering who I am.

Because she almost made me forget myself, for a moment, this woman. Just like Wagner tried to make me forget, tried to make me forget that I am Ruby Miller, I am the phoenix from the ashes, that I am this world's reckoning, nothing less, nothing more.

I am here to take the fucking trash out.

Well, this seems as good a place to start as any.

She sees, too late, what she has done. She has a moment to look at me as I approach, a moment where I see myself reflected in her eyes, and it is I who am the beautiful one, because I wear a crown of fire, and like she says, I am not the bad things that happened to me, I am better, I am purer, I am…

I am…

She screams.

We are on fire.

HELEN

16

H ello, Central?

Yeah, it's Helen. Can you patch me through to Sawtooth, please? No, not Beartooth, *Saw*tooth. No, I don't want to hold, I want you to transfer me, immediately. No, I don't care if he is in a god damn meeting, I don't care if he's taking tea with the pope himself, or Jesus, I want to talk to him NOW.

Thank you.

Yeah, hi.

It's me. Helen.

Yeah, I know you've been expecting me to call. I would have done earlier, when I got the news, only I've been too busy smashing two shades of shit out of things in my office while I try and process this trainwreck.

But I'm calmer now, and I have just one question for you.

What the *fuck*, Mark?

What the actual, fucking fuck?!

Yes, I know I'm shouting! Do you have any idea what

you've *done?* What the blistering fuck was your woman thinking? Wagner? What was she fucking *thinking?*

Initiative, is that it?

Was she trying to show initiative, move up a level, was she after my job?

Well the way I feel today, she can have it, oh, but wait! No she can't, because she's an idiot, and she's dead, and an entire facilty is now out of action, razed to the ground, and over fifty operatives are dead, not to mention three Anomolies, and *worse*, now Ruby is out there in the wild and mad as all fucking hell, and she was pretty fucking mad before! You think Glenns Ferry was bad? How long until she finds herself in a major city, torching everyone and everything in sight? How long do you think we have until she figures out what forest fires are all about, and sets about clearing the world of everything she sees as trouble-some? She isn't a problem to be solved, Mark, we talked about this! She is a force of nature, a fucking demi-god or something like, and you don't coerce, you don't intimidate, you simply steer her in the direction you need and hope she burns herself out, I mean, we *spoke* about this, at great length! Have I been talking to myself, all these months?

Am I a fucking joke to you, is that it?

I don't care about your fucking excuses, Mark, I had a plan! A carefully concocted plan designed to get her on our side. You think she's going to trust anyone, now? Even her own mother? Fuck no! She's going to go on the fucking rampage, is what she's going to do, Mark, and it was your fucking team that started it! Remember that, when we are knee-deep in ash. You should have trusted me. I had a plan.

I had a fucking plan.

Now I need to come up with a new plan. As if I don't have enough to deal with as it is. Time is running out for us, Mark. The Arch...it's been active again. The frequency of it is...accelerating. We don't have long before whatever it is gearing up for, happens. And then we'll have a little more on our plate than a pyromaniac with personality issues, do you understand? We need her on our side, Mark, capiche.

Good.

One last thing. The body Wagner found at the Miller house? Mr. Miller, Ruby's father? Yeah, well, the Mother says Ruby had nothing to do with it. She says, his death is on her. She killed Daddy. Her words, not mine. Apparently, he made her call him that, too. Nice family, huh? Yeah, gross, isn't it. Goes a long way towards explaining some of Ruby's antisocial behaviour, if I was being generous.

Oh, and by the way, you're suspended from duty until I can figure out what to do with you, Mark. I've put Alice in charge in the interim. She should be on her way over, right now.

Let's hope she gets to you before Ruby does, hey?

Now fuck off before I change my mind and have you fired completely.

I've got some thinking to do.

RANDALL

17

Jesus said that all men must be born again.

At least, I think that's what the bible was driving at, I don't know, I haven't read it for a long, long time. But I do remember this passage:

"Jesus answered and said unto him, 'Verily, verily, I say unto thee, except a man be born again, he cannot see the kingdom of God'".

Rebirth comes in different packaging though, and getting a second chance at life isn't always what it's cracked up to be, when all's said and done.

I should know.

Because it doesn't matter how many years go by, or how old I get.

Every night, without fail, I dream of the boy.

THE BOY IS CALLED ELIJAH, and he is somewhere aged between boy and man, nineteen, maybe twenty years old. In my dream he is wearing a white shirt and jeans. There is blood on his shirt, blood that I put there. He sways, unsteady, and his eyes roll back in his head.

Then, he falls.

In my dream, time becomes something soft and thick and slow, like molasses. The boy is falling for what feels like forever, head thrown back, arms out by his sides, like that Jesus statue they've got in Rio de Janeiro, Christ the Redeemer, or like a bird in flight, only he is flying backwards, and downwards, and birds fly up, not down, don't they? He's flying the wrong goddamn way, and its making me sick to my stomach, but there ain't much I can do about it, not now. The dominoes have been tipped, and all I *can* do is watch as one by one, they all fall down, like that nursery rhyme kids sing, the one about roses.

With a crash, he hits the floor. His skull connects with the sidewalk. I hear the sound of bone breaking. I see blood coming out of his nose. I see the whites of his eyes.

I hear people screaming.

I look down at my fist, clenched real tight. The boy twitches, coughs, and then his body goes limp. In the dream, I turn and run, run from what I did, but my feet don't work properly. I don't get anywhere fast. Because you can't escape the things you've done, not when those things are things like this.

In real life, I didn't run. I just stood there until the law came for me. I was only twenty-five. Twenty-five, and I severed an artery in that boy's brain with a single punch. You would think it is impossible to kill a person with a single blow to the head, but it isn't.

I wish it were.

But it isn't.

A one-punch kill, they call it. A single, concentrated moment of violence. Booze and heat and testosterone, all souping up together and working against me. I went to prison for it. My life, and Elijah's, over before it had begun. I got out, after a time, on good behaviour, but I was haunted by Elijah's ghost, and I couldn't stay out of trouble for long, so I ended up back in jail two years later, where I remained. Hell of a waste, in retrospect: two deaths, one dream, over and over again, every night for the rest of my days.

The thing about dreams, is that eventually, you can wake up from them.

The thing about murder, is that you can't.

WHEN THE DREAM gets so bad it wakes me in the early hours of the morning, I know what to do. No point in trying to get back to sleep. Can't put the spilt milk back in the bottle, not now. Sleep is less important the older you get, anyway. Especially when you've spent the last thirty years sleeping on a concrete prison bed. Only thing for it is to get up, brew some coffee, and wait for dawn.

I get dressed. I think maybe today I'll head on up to Borah Peak, see how far up from the trailhead I can get this time before I hit snow and ice. I can see the mountain from my cabin window, or at least, I can see the dark purple shadow of it. The sun will come up behind it soon, and another day will start. Another day of solitude, of quiet. Another day of trying to forget what I did.

Trying, and failing.

I shovel coffee grounds into an old-fashioned stove brewer, and screw the bottom on tight, feeling like I always feel when I do even the most basic of chores around my own house: nervous. Ready. Aware. Since my release, making a cup of coffee for myself feels like a luxury I shouldn't be allowed. I keep looking over my shoulder as I fill the pot, waiting for someone to come up behind me, hit me upside the head, ask me what the fuck my problem is. Inside, you see, there is a pecking order. I was never very high up in that pecking order. I'm a big man, always have been, but after I killed Elijah, I was too scared to use my fists again. In jail, though, fear is not your friend. It gives off a stink, like rotting meat. I got a lot of scars to show for it. I lost the top of my right ear in a fight with my cellmate, once. The prison doc sewed it up in a hurry, and now it looks deformed, ragged. Every time I see it I feel angry, and mean, and smaller than I really am.

Because you can't ever run from what you did, not even when you look in the mirror.

Especially not when you look in the mirror.

The sky lightens with a red glow as I pour steaming hot coffee into a mug. I take it out onto my porch, same as I do every morning. I have an old easy chair out there, with thick blankets to wrap myself in, keep the dawn chill at bay. This cabin belonged to my father, once. He died while I was inside. I feel responsible for that death, too. My father had been a good man, but my crime aged him, turned him bitter and frail. I let so many people down, I can hardly bear to think on it, so I don't. I lock it away. I make coffee. I watch the sun rise. I take it all one step at a time, because there is nothing else I can do.

My brother hung onto the cabin for me, and when I got out, I came straight here. I've been here ever since. It's rent free, a bit cold in the winter, but I get by. I do odd jobs, labouring, anything I can to make a small living. It's not much of a life, but it's a million times better than life in a cell, I can tell you that.

It's a million times better than no life at all.

I should be grateful for it. I *am* grateful for it, but it's a heavy kind of gratitude, mixed up with a whole lot of other feelings, regret being one of them. Getting away from my own regret is hard, these days. Especially after the dreams. It chases me around, an ugly dog nipping at my heels. You can kick the dog, but it'll come back later, so what's the point?

I get comfortable, wait for the sun to rise up over Borah Peak. The sun was the thing I missed most when I was inside. It, like the coffee, feels undeserved, but I wait for it anyway, because this is part of the routine.

The sky gets lighter, and the red turns to a fierce orange, brighter than it usually is at sunrise. There are still stars hanging in the sky, but one by one, they blink out. It's fixing to be a clear, bright day. A good day for walking. Walking is the only thing that brings a measure of peace now that I'm a free man. When you've been confined to small spaces for so long, the big spaces start calling to you, and I answer the call. Most of my days are spent hiking the trails, watching for wildlife, trying to put as much distance between myself and everything else as possible. There's a new route I want to try today, a different side of the peak I want to get up, somehow. Steeper, more technical, but I'll take it slow. One foot in front of the other, till I get to the top.

The sky gets brighter, like a promise of better things to come, and I think to myself: *Maybe tonight. Maybe tonight, if I walk hard enough, if I tire myself out real good, I won't dream.*

Maybe.

It's then that I see the deer, and I realise.

Something is wrong.

THE ANIMAL BURSTS OUT of the treeline in front of my cabin, running in a dead panic, its neck stretched out tight, its legs stiff and primed for speed. I recognise it right away, despite how fast it moves: a pronghorn. I can tell by the strange, bent antlers on its head and the white stripes on its neck.

I sit up. What the fuck is this doing way out here, in the forest? Pronghorns like open space, they are built for speed, like a cheetah. Trees interfere with running, yet here it is, thundering across the space in front of my cabin like the devil's dog is behind it.

I put my coffee down on the porch real careful, and stand up. I listen, head cocked on one side so I can hear better. The deer keeps running, moving faster than I think I've seen anything on this earth with four feet move.

What's it running away from?

My skin prickles.

More movement. I can hear sticks and undergrowth being trampled underfoot, and then more deer burst out of the trees, white-tails this time, a whole herd of them, squealing and charging along in a great rush, driven forward by something, and the sight is so bizarre, so unexpected, that I freeze all over, and then I start to feel deeply, truly afraid.

Because the sky is getting brighter and brighter the whole time, and it hits me, like a punch to the gut. This isn't sunrise. Borah Peak is to one side of the cabin. The orange glow of dawn is coming from the other side.

But the sun doesn't rise in that direction.

I shake myself, take a step forward, heart yammering in my chest, my body tense, straining to listen for anything else out of place. And the more I listen, the more I think I can hear something, rumbling in the distance. Something that sets my teeth on edge, something massive, but I can't...my stupid, slow old brain can't quite figure out what it is.

A flock of birds screams out of the treetops and swarms overhead, a mad rush of wings and panic. Birds of all kinds, not just one species. Small birds, birds of prey, crows, jays, all jammed tight into the air together, like every bird in the forest is packing up and moving out all at once.

Move, Randall, I think.

But I can't. I'm still stuck there on my porch, feet planted to the wood like I'm a goddamned totem pole.

A sea of vermin washes out of the trees, next, and sweeps past my cabin: mice, rats, other things I can't make out as they move too fast. And insects. Thousands of insects, scuttling along as fast as they can, a living carpet of bugs all shifting in the same direction. The sounds they make as they go by are incredible, and I pinch myself on the arm, hard. Am I awake? I think so, but, fuck, I've never seen anything like this!

Then, something breaks out of the treeline that makes the breath stick fast in my throat. Something sandy-couloured, and beautiful, keeping long and low to the ground, moving like silk over skin, deadly, but no less scared for it. I rub my eyes in disbelief.

It's a mountain lion, a fucking mountain lion, running for its life.

Fuck.

Move, Randall! The voice in my head says again, louder this time. *Fucking run, you stupid old bastard!*

Because it clicks then, in my tired brain, and I know suddenly what's coming, just like the animals know what's coming. The sky keeps changing colour, getting brighter and brighter in all the wrong kinds of way, and the rumbling sound gets closer, turns into a roaring noise, like a waterfall, or the ocean, only it ain't either of those things, no, it's worse.

It's fire.

There's a wildfire coming, and me and my cabin are right in its path.

I look down at my feet. I haven't got shoes on, and I have only moments to get out before the fire comes.

But I won't get far without shoes.

Well, shit.

Instinct takes over. I need shoes. There are sneakers inside. I crash into the cabin, grab them, and jam them onto my feet, hopping from foot to foot as I do so, trying to keep some kind of forward motion going, because stopping means dying, and I'm a coward: I don't want to die like this, cooked alive, burned to ash on my own front porch.

Outside, the space above the trees is now a glaring, violent orange, and a huge, stampeding herd of animals of all species flows out of the trees like a river, and there is so much noise, it is indescribable, it feels like the end of days, like something from the bible made real. I leap from my porch, my body creaking and stiff, my joints protesting, and start running too. My station wagon is parked round back. I keep the keys in the ignition, partly because I'm lazy, and partly because there isn't anyone around here who would want to steal it. If I can just make it to the car, I can get some speed on, get the fire behind me. I know how fast wildfires move, and I know I can't outrun it on foot.

I push my body on, and on, and the car comes into view. The orange sky has brightened to a searing, hot white. I can smell smoke now, and I know it won't be long before the heat comes. If I am going to survive, I need to stay ahead of it. The station wagon gets closer, and closer, and I can hear animals screaming, and a small furry shoots out in front of me, and I almost trample it underfoot, stumbling, swearing, wheeling my arms to stay upright, because I can't afford to trip, I can't afford to fall: if I fall, I die.

The car is close, I can reach the handle. I yank open the door, not bothering to close it behind me, because every second is precious, and I turn the key in the ignition, and the car starts, thank Christ.

I put my foot down, and I high-tail it out of there, pulling the door shut as I drive, tyres squealing on the dirt track, animals of all kinds ducking out of the way. I hit something, another deer, I can't help it: it runs straight into me. The station wagon ploughs through it, and it goes under the bonnet with a sickening thump. I can feel the poor creature rolling under my wheels, but I can't stop, there is no time to stop, because stopping means burning alive in my car, and I can't have that.

Then, something huge runs into the road from my right side, and there is no way I can plough through this animal: it's a moose, massive, all muscle and fear, galloping along like a horse at full speed, calling out and making a desperate lowing sound as it runs. If I hit that, my car will be a write-off. I slam my foot on the brakes desperately, bringing it to a stop seconds before hitting the animal, stalling the station wagon. The moose swerves to avoid me, and keeps charging down the road. The sky around me is full of floating, burning ash, carried on a wind that hadn't been there minutes before. Glowing curls of ash drift down and land on my windscreen. Swearing, I turn the key, over and over again, hammering the steering wheel in desperation with the palm of my other hand, the engine coughing but not starting, and I shoot a look in my rear-view mirror to see how far behind me the wildfire is, and...

And I see something.

Something impossible.

Something that shouldn't... be.

It's a girl, tall, and naked.

She walks slowly, arms held out to either side of her

just like Elijah's arms were held out, like the arms of a crucifix, in my dreams. Like a bird spreading its wings. Flames shoot out of every part of her, roaring, screaming, furious fire that dances and sings, and she is in the middle of it, walking along like it's a clear spring day, and I start to cough, my eyes streaming hot tears down my face, because the smoke is getting thicker, but I can't stop looking at her, this thing, this girl, and then, as she gets closer, impossibly, I understand: the fire isn't coming *from* her. It isn't coming *out* of her.

She *is* the fire.

And she's walking towards me.

Oh God, she's walking towards me and everything around her is burning! Is she laughing? Her mouth is open, stretched wide, but from here, I can't tell what's coming out of it.

GO, RANDALL!

My subconscious really wants to keep me alive.

I turn the key again, almost blind now from the glare of the blaze, and the smoke. The engine starts. My foot slams down to the metal.

I drive for my life.

I make it three miles to the outskirts of the forest before the station wagon gives out, engine shuddering to a stop. Is it enough? I don't sit around to think about it. It's taken me far enough that I can see a large, green reservoir up ahead, and I know what I need to do.

The girl on fire is behind me, but there is water in front of me.

I run for the reservoir.

18

I'm standing in water, up to my waist in it, shivering, breath coming fast and shallow, and I am watching the world burn.

The sky isn't bright anymore. Massive, black clouds boil up from the crackling forest and blot out the sun, which has risen from behind the mountain and gone to bed again in the smoke. Towering flames chase after the smog, eating everything in their path. From here, it looks like hell, like those old paintings of it you see in museums and in books. Every now and then, the smoke and the fire shift direction, pushed around by the wind, and I can see the bones of trees against the glow. The air is hot, and stinks. It's hard getting harder and harder to breathe. I take off my shirt with numb fingers, and soak it in the water of the reservoir, tying it back over my mouth like a mask, trying to stop any more fumes from getting into my lungs.

The fire roars closer all the time, like a freight train coming, the sound hurting my ears, it's so loud, and I am trapped, the reservoir behind me, everything else burning to shit out in front of me. I hold to a weak hope that the water keeps me safe. I am not the only one with the same idea: a steady stream of wildlife joins me in the reservoir, a dog, a racoon, more deer and rats, and just when I think life can't get any more surreal, the moose I saw earlier surges out of the fog like a charging stallion and crashes into the lake not ten feet away from me, submerging itself up to its neck and treading water as it waits for the fire to pass us by. If you'd have told me yesterday that I'd be taking a cold bath with a moose the next morning, I would have laughed at you. At this point, I am so exhausted I can't react. The animal is not interested in me, only in what's coming for us.

Because we are being hunted, and we both know it.

And then, as if on cue, she appears. The girl on fire. Walking out of the blaze, slow and stately, crown of flames glowing around her bald head. She knows we are here. She is coming for us, body pulsing with a hot, bright outline of white. She wants us to burn, and it shows on her face. She is beautiful, and relentless, and completely fucking terrifying.

She means to walk right into the water, I can tell.

Turning, desperate, I see a small, rocky outcrop out in the middle of the reservoir. A tiny island, big enough to climb up onto, sitting there as if it had been left just for me. A good distance away, not an easy swim, but surrounded by water. There is no way the fire can reach me there, not unless it can cross water, and fire doesn't work like that, I'm pretty sure of it.

It's been a long time since I had a swim.

I wade further into the lake until the water reaches my shoulders. There is something dancing in the air, now, aside from the noise of the fire and the devastation all around.

It's the sound of a girl, laughing.

I start swimming.

❦

I DRAG my body through the water in a painful front crawl, trying to remember how this works, trying to remember how keen a swimmer I was when I was a kid. One arm down, drag it through the water. Other arm out, and down, drag that back too. Don't forget to kick, and breathe. Arms, legs, breathe. Arms, legs, breathe.

I swim for what feels like a whole lifetime, pausing to rest only once, when cramp bites my legs. It is so sudden I can't help it: I come to a dead halt, try and grab my calves with my hands, and almost drown in the process.

The cramp bites again, and I flail and cry out, head going under, swallowing a bitter lungful of water. Coughing and spluttering, I surface, and the pain is devastating, but I can't give into it. I don't need legs, I have arms, and those arms need to get me out of this fucking lake right now.

But I'm tired, I think. *I'm so fucking tired.*

Elijah wasn't tired, the voice in the back of my mind says, reasonably. *Elijah was young, and had his whole life ahead of him, and yet you murdered him anyway.*

Tired? The voice goes on, and is it my imagination, or can I hear contempt there?

Tired?

Don't be such a fucking coward, Randall. Swim! SWIM!

Using only my arms to drag me through the water, I strike out again, my body locked up in agony, legs useless from the cramp. A panicky instinct forces me to look back once, just to make sure the girl isn't close enough to hurt me. And it feels like my whole life I've been doing this, looking over my shoulder to see what's coming for me, and

I'm angry suddenly, angry at the voice in my head for pushing me on when really, I've got nothing left to live for. But that doesn't seem to bother the voice. The voice wants me to live, wretched and old and tired as I am.

But the girl on fire wants me to die.

And I can see her, walking into the lake.

The water doesn't frighten her like I hoped it would, not one bit.

The water doesn't put out her fire, either. Impossible, but there we have it.

The girl walks into the water, and the fire still burns.

A massive cloud of steam erupts all around her as the reservoir starts to bubble, and hiss.

The girl on fire is burning the water clean away.

She doesn't care about nature, what should and shouldn't happen.

She makes her own rules.

And now I have a new problem. I won't burn to death, but if I stay here much longer, paddling on the spot like a dog, I'll boil, like a crab in a pot.

No more looking back, not now. I drag myself along, desperate, eyes fixed on the island. I can feel the water warming up around me. I can feel fish swimming up against my legs, swimming away from the heat, frantic, like the birds in the sky earlier. I can feel other things under the surface, but I don't have time to guess at what they are, only that they, like me, are trying to survive.

Hell, I keep thinking, over and over. *I'm in hell.*

And the water gets hotter and hotter, because that's what I deserve.

Then, amazingly, my hand strikes rock, and I realise that it's the island, I've made it, I've gone and made it, and I use the last of my strength to pull myself onto a ledge, trying despite everything to stay alive and knowing it won't do any good, because, in the end, what's the point? You can't outrun the things that scare you the most, and sooner or later, they'll catch up to you, and eat you up, and you'll burn, just like you deserve to.

I feel myself blacking out, the world in flames slipping away.

My last, conscious hope is that Elijah isn't there in the darkness, waiting for me. Because I need, so desperately, to sleep.

To sleep, and not to dream.

When I wake up, the lake has boiled dry.

Hungry fire stretches out across the horizon, circling my world from end to end. Groggy, I rub my eyes, and I can see helicopters and planes in the distance, dumping water on the flames. Where from, I don't know, because this reservoir is only a great bare, cracked basin of rock now, and I am on a tiny stone shelf sticking out of it like a thumb, high up in the middle. The air tastes like ash, and there are dead things all over the bed of the lake. Fish, birds, animals. If I look, I can make out what is left of the moose, its legs stuck out from a swollen belly, head and antlers twisted to one side. The contorted skeletons of pines cover the land behind the reservoir with black, bony stalks, and I realise that my cabin, the only home I had outside of prison, has gone, burned to charcoal.

And yet I'm still alive, like some cruel fucking joke.

I roll over onto my front. And see her.

A naked woman, sitting next to me on the rock shelf, waiting.

I stare at her in horror, but I can't run. There is nothing left in me, no strength, no will, no fight. I'm alive, but I would rather not be. The voice in my head can go fuck itself. This is it, for me. I don't want to live in a world where a human woman can make things burn the way this one does.

And yet the woman who makes fire come out of her skin just sits there, naked as the day she was born, picking at her fingernails as if nothing is out of the ordinary.

'Don't panic,' she says, bitterly. 'I couldn't kill you even if I wanted to, not now.'

She lifts a hand, palm to the sky, and a tiny blue flame ripples across her skin, flares briefly, then dies. She tries it again, and I flinch, but again the flame snuffs out.

'I'm clean out of fire,' she says, and then coughs. I can see blood on her lips. Not red, or bright, but brown, and sticky. Like it's mixed with ash. She pauses in the act of wiping it away, frowning. Then, she spits. A yellow tooth lands on the rock shelf right in front of me. She doesn't seem upset by this. I notice other gaps in her teeth, and her gums look like they are bleeding.

It's like she is decaying, somehow, from the inside out.

The girl who isn't on fire seems to want to talk.

'You know, most people want to know how I do it. Where the flames come from.'

I continue to stare at her, thinking, *what difference does it make, knowing how she does it? Dead is dead and burned is burned.* Finding out the 'how' won't stop the 'why'.

She continues. 'When this first happened to me, I was in a car crash. Whole car went up like a fireball. My cherry red Pontiac Bonneville. My baby. All my worldly savings I spent on that car, and it blew up with me inside. But, I survived. Woke up like brand new. Better than brand new. Invincible. I was shot, hit on the head by a fire extinguisher, hit by a goddamn train.' She laughs, and there is a rattle in her chest like blood or fluid.

'I came out of everything without a scratch on my body. Like a newborn. And the fire...it just got hungrier and hungrier.' She shrugs, weary. 'And now...well, look at me. I don't know what's happening. Bits and pieces of me falling off everywhere.' She gestures to her ankle, and I see a great, festering sore there, more of a hole, actually, same size as an apple, and through it, I can just about make out bone. She jams a finger into the sore, wiggles it around, experimenting with its depth. I feel queasy watching her, and struggle to keep the contents of my stomach under lock and key.

'I guess all good things have to come to an end sooner or later,' She sighs, tapping her fingernail on her open ankle bone. 'God fuck it, though. I wish it had lasted longer. I had so much more to do.'

I open my mouth, trying to make words come out of it, but I've got nothing. I am as dry as the lake bed all around. I could try and run from the crazy bitch, but where would I go? Everything around me is wasteland or fire.

The girl continues, picking at her fingernails, and I see one of them come away from the nailbed. Underneath the skin is black, like it is rotting. She rips it off and throws it away like it is nothing, and starts working on the next.

'And then,' she says, remembering something. 'Then there was the town of Glenns Ferry. They said it was an industrial accident, that a cargo train blew up because of a...what was it now? Oh, right, yeah. A malfunction in a container. I mean, did they expect people to believe that horsehit?'

Glenns Ferry. Pain grips my heart. I was inside at the time, but I saw it on the news. All of America knows about Glenn's Ferry. A whole town, wiped off the map by an explosion. Worst industrial accident in America's history, the TV said.

I work my throat, and the words finally come out of me, hoarse and weak.

'Was that you?'

The woman nods. 'Yeah that was me.' She grins, suddenly, and holds out a hand, giggling.

'Hi. I'm Ruby Miller. And I'm a mass murderer. Call me the Joker, only with tits.' This sets her off laughing, which makes her cough, which makes her spit blood again.

I lower my head.

'My cousin lived in Glenns Ferry,' I say, blankly staring at the ground. 'My favourite cousin. We used to...we used to play blackjack until dawn when I was a kid. He could...'

I stop, overcome.

Ruby sighs, and lays back on the barren shore, her head resting in her hands, which she laces together to form a pillow.

'Well, I wish I could tell you I was sorry, friend,' she says, in a level voice that is without remorse. 'But I'm not. I'm not much of anything, anymore.'

And I suddenly recognise what I'm listening to. I recognise it, because I used to be it. I was Ruby, all those years ago when I punched Elijah in the head and killed him right there on the sidewalk. Angry, hurting, unable to control it. Just wanting to rip the world down bit by bit, because I didn't know what else to do. Afterwards, I was like this: flat. Empty. The remorse didn't get me right away, oh no. It took years of staring at a wall, years of wondering when my cell mate was going to kill me in my sleep.

Guilt is a slow-growing flower.

She rolls over, stretches out like she is sunbathing, and I look at her, at the tattoo on her scalp. It's a phoenix, wings outstretched, curling around her skull protectively. I think again of all the inmates I've seen over the years, wearing their tattoos like protective armour, and how tattoos are like a pedigree on the inside, whether it's a name, or a symbol, or a slogan, or the face of someone you love. I look down at the insides of my wrists, where I have had the same name inked twice, one for each side of my body:

Elijah.

Elijah.

Because I was young, and stupid, and I wore my crime like a badge, like an idiot. Until the flower bloomed.

And I get it, looking at her. She is proud of her pain, and her power. In her eyes, she is a Phoenix, risen from ashes to exact revenge for whatever hurt her in the past, because you can tell she's been hurt. Kids this young don't swagger like she does unless they're hiding something they're ashamed of. I should know. Just like I know she isn't going to stop destroying things until she literally falls apart at the seams. The fire is her friend. She's already killed hundreds upon hundreds of people, and just because she's tired now, doesn't mean she won't do it again.

She'll keep doing it until she can't, because sometimes, the anger is all there is.

I rest back on my hands, and feel something brush against my skin. I explore it with tingling, reaching fingers.

It's a large, sharp rock, the size of my fist.

It only took one blow to kill Elijah.

I'm not as young and strong as I once was, but if I can get close enough, the stone could do for Ruby what my fist did to Elijah years before. She said herself that she is weak, and out of fire. And her body is crumbling, exhausted by her rampage.

Is this why I'm alive? I think. *Some divine purpose?*

Some unlikely fucking hero.

'You burned my house down,' I say, quietly, staring at the horizon once more. 'Burned a lot of houses down, I imagine.'

'Yeah,' Ruby says, and pushes up from the ground, spits again. 'I know.' Another tooth goes flying through the air, landing in the cracked bed of the reservoir, right next to the cooked carcass of a large fish.

'If it makes you feel any better,' she continues, wiping her mouth with the back of her hand, 'People are all trash, anyway. A world full of trash people, all walking around, messing up everything they touch. If I don't do it, burn things down, someone else will, eventually. You know that.' She peels off another fingernail, and flicks it into the empty lake. 'Trash people,' she repeats, and there is a rage there under her tiredness. 'It makes my fucking skin crawl.'

'You've got a pretty bleak view of the world, Miss,' I say, but as much as my heart goes out to her, and it does, suddenly, I know that I'm about to do the right thing.

She laughs, then sighs. 'Yeah, well,' she says. 'You would too, if you were me.'

And I decide I can't stand seeing her naked like this in front of me anymore. If I'm going to kill her, I'll make sure she's partway covered, at least. That feels like the most... respectful thing to do. I unwrap the shirt that I've been using as a mask from my neck, shake it out, and hand it to her, slowly.

She looks at it, then shrugs. She takes it, and puts it on. Something shifts in the atmosphere between us. Something in the way she holds herself, something in how brittle she feels as she talks.

And then, because I got nothing better to do than give advice to a mass-murdering freak of nature before I execute her, I decide to tell her something. I watch the smoke choking up the sky, and watch the helicopters buzzing in the distance like angry bees, and it comes out. Just slips out, like I was kept alive for the sole purpose of sitting here, and saying this.

'Seems to me,' I say, and my mouth is dry, so I lick my lips, and try again. 'Seems to me that all this hate is curdling your insides, Ruby. I don't know much, but I do know this: you gotta let it go. You can't keep punishing the world because you're angry.'

'Nice try, old man,' Ruby says, amused. 'But someone else tried to pull that compassionate shit on me only a little while ago, and it didn't stick, it didn't stick at all. She's in the air now, floating around somewhere. Dust. I fried her good and hard.'

'Randall,' I reply. 'My name's Randall.'

'Well, Randall, let me tell you a story,' Ruby continues, and a thin, weak line of blue fire works its way along the backs of her fingers.

19

She starts talking. I grip the rock hard in my hand. I should listen to what she is saying, I owe her that much at least, but I can't. All I can hear is the voice in the back of my head, and it says one thing, over and over.

Kill her.

Kill her.

Kill her.

I'm on my feet. She isn't far away. She sees me get up, stops talking, eyes narrowing.

'What's your game, Randall?' she says, suspicious, and I stumble closer to her, the rock held tight behind my back.

She starts rising to her own feet, slowly. It's now, or never. I come for her, the rock held high. I bring it down, hard, but she is too fast, she's on her feet properly, standing tall, and her hand flies up, and catches my wrist.

We stand there, locked together in a weak, pathetic struggle, an old man and a young girl, both killers, both victims of our own worst nature, and our eyes meet.

'I can't die, you know,' she says, and then, she lets go of

my wrist. I have a split moment to catch her eyes, glowing bright and red, and to realise that she has found just enough anger left to defend herself. She has found a hidden well-spring inside of her.

Not yet, old man, I tell myself. *Not yet.*

But Ruby cannot hear the voice. Ruby has her own voice, and it is telling her to burn.

She wraps her arms around me, tight, a terrible, crushing embrace, and I can feel power throbbing in every part of her skinny, long body, and then, well.

Then there is nothing else but fire.

AND THEN, we open our eyes.

'I...don't understand,' says Ruby, eyes wide, and she lets go of me, stumbling back.

Neither do I.

Because I'm still alive.

And I didn't burn.

Told you, the voice in the back of my mind says, cheerfully.

Ruby sits down suddenly on the ground, and her nose starts to bleed. It pours out of her in twin, crimson ropes, dripping onto the floor and puddling all around her.

'If you keep bleeding like that, you'll fill the lake up again,' I say, stupidly.

'You didn't burn,' she said, in disbelief, and just like that, she looks like the child she must have been once, lost, and confused, and alone. Not like a mass murderer at all.

Well, we were all children once, I suppose.

I sit on the shelf next to Ruby, take off my vest, and hand it to her. She flinches from me, but I persist. After a moment or two of me holding it out, refusing to budge, she takes it. She uses it to stem the flow of blood from her nose, shivering, her whole world shaken.

And around us, without warning, it starts to rain.

I hear a hissing noise. I frown, then fix on the source of the noise, see steam coming off of Ruby's body. The rain is evaporating as it hits her skin. She sucks in a sharp breath. She is in pain.

No, not evaporating...dissolving.

The rain is dissolving the skin clean off her body.

Her eyes widen. She stares at the flesh on her arms, which bubble and fizz like a freshly popped soda. Her lip quivers, and she looks up at me with a mixture of panic and terror. A child, nothing more. A damaged, hurt child.

'What's happening to me?' She whispers, and it's hard to feel sorry for the person who single-handedly took Glenns Ferry off the map, who burned my cousin to ash, destroyed hundreds of miles of forest and parkland wildlife and infrastructure and reduced my only home to charcoal, but I managed it, somehow. I *do* feel sorry for her. I watch as another tooth falls out of her mouth. She sputters, coughs, and two more fly loose, scattering to the ground. I see holes in them, her teeth are honeycombed with rot. Her nosebleed starts up again, heavier, clotted, sticky and disgusting. Meanwhile, the skin on her shoulders, neck, and back is coming up in large, yellowish blisters as the rain comes down harder, soaking the world as fast as it burned. The blisters burst, one by one, little milky explosions going off all over, and Ruby cries out in agony. I see her shoulder blades suddenly through her skin, white and shocking, and I see that her flesh is melting clean away, as if the rain is acid, and I think, dumb as a rock trying to catch up with a rabbit, *Freak storm? Pollution? Acid rain?* But...but I can see droplets of water trembling fresh upon my own skin, and I am just fine, nothing is happening to me, so it *can't* be acid, it must be something to do with Ruby.

What is happening to her?

I don't know. I don't know anything, I don't know what she is, or why her body is suddenly falling apart, or how to help her. I don't know what else to do, except watch, like this is a slowed down movie on screen in front of me, a show only two of us have a ticket for.

Her ears start to bleed. The sore in her ankle opens up, gradually consuming her entire foot and most of her lower leg. Another one makes short work of her left kneecap. Most of the skin on her once beautiful face has now sloughed off. Her hands are bone, and she holds them up in front of her, turning them over and over, chest heaving even as it dissolves.

'I don't understand…' She makes a strangled, gurgling sound, falling backwards, laying flat out so that her face is turned directly up to the sky. Her tears get lost in the rain, and moments later, as I sit frozen in disbelief and horror, her eyes sink inwards, turning to mush and running down the yellow contours of her exposed skull in rivulets.

There is a moment where the dying girl summons enough strength to grab a hold of my wrist with one skeletal hand, a desperate blind, grasping moment where she latches onto me, her bony fingertips scoring red marks in my arm, and then her grip tightens, her hands fall to the earth, and just like that, all that is left of Ruby Miller, the girl on fire, the angry kid who wanted to burn down the world and reshape it in her image, is a slowly spreading pool of slurry, out of which, yellow bones rise up, looking like the bones of the scorched trees she has left in her wake, over on the shore.

20

W*ell, I suppose that solves that problem,* I think, and the rain keeps falling, soaking me through, cleansing the earth of Ruby's bitterness.

And I guess I'm safer now she's gone, and so is the rest of the world, but I feel heavy with things I don't fully understand, like how bad a person's life has to be for them to turn into what she turned into, and what a shame it was that she couldn't have found a friend or something to steer her right whilst she was so young.

And then I remember, as I sit watching vigil over her bones, I remember the tattoo on her scalp. The phoenix. Just like the bible, I don't recall much about history, but I do remember hearing about the legend of the phoenix once when I was inside. An old documentary on the Discovery channel, something about ancient civilisations, and what did it say? Something about…

Yeah, that was it.

Rebirth.

The bird dies, decays, and is reborn. A cycle, like nature in fall, like trees losing their leaves, blooms dying on the vine, only to come back again next year, fresh and new, ready to start the whole thing all over.

Guilt is a slow-growing flower.

A different flower starts growing in my mind. An idea.

I should have ignored it.

But I don't. Because I believe in second chances, and third, and fourth, and as many chances as it takes for a person to realise how to live properly, how to overcome, a chance I never had…

Or is *this* my second chance?

Anyhow, it seems rude to leave her laying out there like that, all exposed to the elements. I wouldn't like it, if it were me. My remains left uncovered, unmarked. I'd want someone to cover me over while I slept, so this is what I do for Ruby. I collect rocks from the banks of the tiny shelf in the middle of the lake, and I pile them up and over her body. I make a tomb for her, I make a stone blanket, I tuck her in, this kid, wondering if her Daddy ever did that for her, knowing somehow without knowing *how* I know, that he didn't.

Then I sit, and wait.

For what, I don't really know.

But for something.

Something.

❦

THE RAIN DRIES UP, eventually. The heavy thick clouds hanging overhead break up, drift away as a wind picks up. Blue sky emerges like freshly washed sheets from behind them, and the air smells of wet ash, of bloated, dead things, of charred wasteland. I can still hear helicopters in the distance, putting out the remnants of fire the weather didn't get to.

The sun breaks out. It's weak, but warm on my face.

It falls upon Ruby's tomb, and a faint mist rises from the stones as the rainwater evaporates.

And as I watch, knowing in my heart that something is about to happen, knowing that my life has changed now, beyond recall, and realising that maybe, maybe that's okay, because it's better than sitting in my cabin on a mountainside waiting for dreams of Elijah to come, anything is better than that, as I sit there, my insides turning over and over in anticipation, I see a faint orange glow coming from inside the makeshift tomb, I see that glow flicker and then get stronger and more steady, like a sunrise coming up over Borah Peak, and I smile. The idea was a good one.

Ruby Miller is about to be reborn.

Pain.

And then, nothing. Only darkness. Only regret.

I've been here before.

This is me, dying, only I'm not dead.

I'm...I don't know what I am.

But I'm still here.

And it was like it was, back when I crashed my car, only stronger this time, this feeling of new life, new possibilities. I was falling apart, my body was melting away like snow in the sun, but my new skin feels soft, and clean, and warm, and healthy, and when I open my new eyes, I can see a brilliant blue sky through cracks in a stone ceiling above me.

I can see sky, and I can feel my heart beating again, hear the sound of my own ragged, virgin breath, but more importantly, most important of all, I can feel fire in my veins and in my blood and in my heart and I embrace it, it embraces me, that wonderful, beautiful heat, and this time, it's going to be different, this time I am not going to waste what I've been given, this time, I am going to set things straight, correct the balance, take out the trash.

And as I remember how to laugh, as it bubbles out of me like rich, warm lava, I think, fiercely:

I am the eye of the fucking storm.
I am the Phoenix from the ashes.
Cower before me, motherfuckers.
Because I feel better than ever.

RUBY WILL RETURN IN BLAZE

ABOUT THE AUTHOR

Gemma Amor is the Bram Stoker Award nominated author of *DEAR LAURA*, *CRUEL WORKS OF NATURE*, *THESE WOUNDS WE MAKE* and *WHITE PINES*.

She is also a podcaster, illustrator and voice actor, and is based in Bristol, in the U.K.

Many of her stories have been adapted into audio dramas by the wildly popular NoSleep Podcast, and her work also features on shows like Shadows at the Door, Creepy, and The Grey Rooms podcast.

She is the co-creator, writer and voice actor for horror-comedy podcast Calling Darkness, which also stars Kate Siegel. Her next books are the dark fantasy novella *GIRL ON FIRE*, travel-horror collection *PLACES WE FEAR TO TREAD*, and the hotly anticipated charity anthology *WE ARE WOLVES*.

Heavily influenced by classical literature, gothic romance, tragedy and heroism, she is most at home in front of a fire with a single malt and a dog-eared copy of anything by Angela Carter.

gemmammorauthor.com
Facebook.com/littlescarystories
Twitter.com/manylittlewords
Instagram.com/manylittlewords

Printed in Great Britain
by Amazon